MW01278316

Beyond Life

Beyond Life

Victoria Helmink

Filidh Publishing

Copyright © 2018 by Victoria Helmink
www.victoriahelmink.com

All rights reserved. This book or any portion thereof may not be reproduced or used in any manner whatsoever without the express written permission of the publisher except for the use of brief quotations in a book review or scholarly journal.

First Printing: 2018

ISBN 978-1-927848-36-4

Filidh Publishing
www.filidhbooks.com

Dedication

To my amazing family and friends.

Without your encouragement and support, this book
would not have made it out into the world.

Acknowledgements

To my readers. Thank you for sharing this adventure with me. Having this book in your hands is a dream come true.

Mom – thank you for all of your guidance and love. You taught me to embrace my creativity, and chase my dreams.

Zoe – without you, this book would still be a file gathering dust in the depths of my computer. Thank you for helping me bring my wish to life.

Kenton – thank you for sharing your passion for writing. You keep me inspired.

Dooley – thank you for being right…again.

Akasha – thank you for always listening to my ideas, and sharing my excitement.

To the many others I have not named (I wish I could name you all), thank you!

Beyond Life

One...

"Children are the hands by which we take hold of heaven."
– Henry Ward Breecher

On a dark suburban street, a flame flickered to life under the protection of a man's hand, licking at the paper of his cigarette. A weary inhale flared the dull embers into a lively glow, illuminating his stark features with harsh shadows. Tipping his head back, he exhaled the smoke, watching it disperse among the raindrops. Nicotine was certainly one of the more soothing human creations.

Asmodeus took another long drag from the cigarette, smiling grimly as the wind snatched the smoke away from his lips as he exhaled again. Shifting his weight, he leaned a shoulder against the lamppost. He did not feel the cold, despite the winter wind pulling at his trench coat.

His eyes narrowed sharply as a car turned the corner, announcing its arrival with an obnoxious backfire. At ten past seven, the father was coming home later than usual. The beat-up station wagon swerved out of the turn haphazardly before finally straightening, and speeding down the road. With a grating screech, the car came to a stop at a careless angle in the driveway across the street. Asmodeus watched the man stumble from the car, and sneered in disgust. He could smell the stench of violence clinging to the man. To his altered perception, the man's aggression stunk as strongly as the liquor on his breath. Irritably, Asmodeus chewed his cigarette, watching the drunk man stagger into the small house. The door slammed behind him.

How many nights had he been forced to stand guard in this modern ghetto, and watch the same events unfold? Too many, and each had been the same. An argument, frequently followed by the wife's pain-filled cries. It seemed the neighbors had stopped listening years ago, too busy with their own problems to be concerned with the ones next door. Taking another drag of his cigarette, Asmodeus watched the two silhouettes in the living room window.

Protect the kid; those were his orders. After years of skillful service, Gabrielle mocked his abilities, and tasked him with babysitting duty. It was no secret that Azriel would have been better suited for this assignment. However, it seemed Asmodeus had tested Gabrielle's patience too long, and was overdue for punishment.

An understanding of why this kid deserved his own astral bodyguard still eluded Asmodeus. By all appearances the boy was ordinary. In fact, with dark hair that hung in his eyes, his lanky height, and typical teenage angst, the kid was distinctly average. He was another unlucky teenager slogging through the struggles of youth.

Asmodeus sighed impatiently, allowing himself to be distracted by a young couple walking down the street, laughing at their private jokes. His bleak mood only worsened as he bitterly watched their progress towards him. As they approached their joviality sobered, instinctively sensing his angry presence. In spite of passing within inches of him, their searching eyes overlooked him. Nervously they hurried on and unlocked their front door, only relaxing as they entered the familiarity of their home.

With his distraction gone, Asmodeus turned his attention back to his task. Even from across the street, he could hear the muffled shouting of the father. It looked like the fight was starting early tonight. He considered intervening to calm them, but felt no great urgency. Usually, the father settled down after shouting himself to the point of exhaustion. Besides, he couldn't help but feed off the anger flowing from the husband.

As the argument intensified, the wife shook her head, and turned to retreat upstairs. Not willing to be ignored, the husband grabbed her arm. Roughly, he spun her back to face him, striking her across the cheek as he did so.

Taking that as his cue, Asmodeus exhaled a rush of smoke, and flicked the butt of the cigarette to the ground, crushing it underfoot. He sauntered across the street, his footsteps silent on the concrete. He soothed his impatience as he approached the living room window, knowing that he would only worsen the situation otherwise. "Damn it." He muttered as he observed the chaos unfolding inside. He had underestimated how quickly the situation would escalate.

The woman crouched in the corner of the room with a split lip, and cried as she cradled her limp arm. Between them stood their son, who was boldly staring down his father. Asmodeus couldn't help but smirk. Waves of dark fury flowed from the boy in equal portion to his father. Like father, like son. Clearly, tempers ran in this family. Despite his bravado, Asmodeus saw the boy falter as his father fixed his gaze on him.

Asmodeus sensed the blow before it came, and watched the boy stumble from the impact. Stunned, the boy wavered, and then he fell back, striking his head on the corner of the coffee table.

Time seemed to slow, as Asmodeus stood captivated, his eyes locked with the boy's as he crumbled. The boy's surprised expression faded as his eyes closed. He lay motionless, a thin line of blood forming where he had struck his head.

"Aidan!" The mother screamed, but he did not stir.

Asmodeus chewed the end of his cigarette. It never boded well for a human when they caught a glimpse of him. Gabrielle would not be pleased.

Two...

*"No one can confidently say that
he will still be living tomorrow."*
– Euripides

An Hour Earlier...

"Have you read Act One yet?"

"I finished it before you called," Aidan answered as he glanced at the pages of Hamlet spread out on his bed.

"And what did you think?" Jazmine asked.

"Reading and understanding are two very different things." His tone betrayed his foul mood. "Why do we have to read this junk? It's not even relevant to real life."

"It's relevant because it affects your grade."

"Only because someone decided it had to." He complained.

Jazmine was undeterred by his frustration. Where he was quick to anger, she was calm, and seemed to have endless patience. "Come on, it's only a few months until graduation, and then we are off to college where we can study what we want."

"And we can move to the city." He said with reverence.

Academically, college was not very interesting to him, what Aidan craved was freedom from his father. College wasn't something he would have dreamed of prior to Jazmine's help. He knew that without her, his grades wouldn't have even garnered a glance from college admissions departments. However, with Jazmine's encouragement, and tutoring, he had managed to boost his grades enough to gain an acceptance letter to the same college as her. Now he was eagerly counting down the days until school finished, and they left for the city together.

Jazmine laughed, pleased by his enthusiasm. "So eager to move away from home." She commented. "Speaking of home... when are you going to introduce me to your parents?"

Aidan cringed at the question, gripping his cell phone a little tighter. He rested his head heavily on the pillows, rubbing his forehead.

"Soon, babe." He whispered into the phone, trying to appease her.

"You've been saying that for five months now, Aidan. Do they even know about us?" Jazmine asked, the concern evident in her voice.

"Of course, they do, Jazz. It's just that they are... different." He didn't mind the idea of Jazz meeting his Mom, in fact, he suspected that they would get along well, but the thought of introducing her to his father was terrifying.

"Hon, all parents are different. But I still want to meet them." She responded confidently. "Besides, I'm not afraid of different."

"All right, I'll set it up with my Mom." Aidan conceded, hoping they could plan for a time when his father wouldn't be home. Reminded now of his father, he glanced at the time. 7:08pm. "I have to go, babe." Outside he heard a car backfire, and he tensed automatically.

"Okay. Love you." Jazz said, followed by an expectant silence.

He hesitated for a moment, the words catching in his throat. Sighing, he whispered into the phone. "Night, babe. Sweet dreams." He lingered on the phone, only hanging up after she did. Mentally he chided himself for once again not being able to say the words he already felt. He didn't doubt that he loved her, but the fear that something would go wrong as soon as he admitted it paralyzed him. His stomach gave an anxious twist as he wondered how long she would wait to hear those three words before giving up on him entirely.

Aidan sat up slowly, hearing the front door slam as his father came in. He couldn't quite make out his mom's timid greeting, but he listened intently for a response. The rumble of his father's voice made his stomach clench, and he rolled out of bed, going to the doorway of his room. He swore under his breath at his father as the yelling started. From the safety of the room, it was easy to imagine brave words to say to him. He had played the hero countless times in his imagination.

For a moment he hesitated, his hand resting on the door handle. If he stayed here, he wouldn't have to get involved. He'd likely be left alone, safe, and unharmed. If he intervened, he would save his mom some pain. In the next room, he could hear a thud, and a muffled cry.

Pulling open the door, he stepped into the hallway, and turned the corner into the living room.

Adrenaline coursed through his systems as he caught sight of his mom crouched in the corner of the room, with a split lip. Judging from the way she held her limp arm, it was broken again. His father Tyler stood across from her, yelling about her incompetence.

Aidan's hands balled into fists, and he stepped in front of his mother. "Leave her alone." He said, trying to muster some strength into his voice. Despite his bravado, he could feel the tremble of his muscles, and hoped the tyrant in front of him wouldn't notice. His gaze settled on his father's chin, unable to meet his gaze without flinching.

"Stay out of this, boy!" Tyler hissed through gritted teeth, his temper only flaring more at the confrontation. His hand closed into a fist, and the blow intended for his wife fell on Aidan instead.

Aidan reeled from the blow as his father's fist connected with his cheek. He tried to recover his balance, but staggered, still stunned by the impact. Through his pain blurred vision, he saw the edge of the coffee table rising to meet him. The corner struck the side of his head near the temple. The impact reverberated down his spine. Without feeling, he slid the rest of the way to the ground, his head settling onto the carpet. He barely felt the blows that followed.

A dull sense of finality comforted him as the blackness started to overtake him. As his vision darkened, he could make out the blurred silhouette of a man through the living room window. Under the shadow of the fedora, he could make out unforgiving blue eyes. They were ice blue, and just as cold.

It was strange that the man didn't try to help, despite going out of his way to peer through their window. He couldn't hear his mom screaming anymore, so maybe this was it. Then there was blackness, and no more thought.

~~~~~~~~~

A light breeze blew over Aidan's arms, sending a chill through him. He opened his eyes, and winced as the lights of emergency vehicles assaulted his eyes. Two ambulances, and two police cars lined the sidewalk in front of his house. Beyond the police cars, the neighbors were gathered in small groups, playing witness to the excitement. In hushed tones, they gossiped about past incidents at the house.

It was strange that he hadn't heard the blare of sirens announcing the emergency vehicles' arrival. In fact, he couldn't even remember how he had gotten outside. He gingerly touched his temple, worried about how hard he had hit his head. The memory of the events seemed beyond the grasp of his memory.

Aidan noticed his father sitting in one of the police cruisers. He couldn't help, but shiver at Tyler's scowl, and quickly looked away as his father glanced in his general direction. Taking a deep breath, he tried to quiet his fear. The cops were here; his Dad would have to leave them alone for now. Near the police car, two officers were speaking, and making notes.

Taking a few steps towards the cruiser, Aidan tried to listen to the conversation. As he moved closer, the air started to thicken as if a thunderstorm was gathering overhead. Aidan shivered with discomfort, and quickly retreated.

As he moved away from the police car, the atmosphere started to buzz with activity. Aidan hesitated, unfamiliar with the strange new sensations. He brushed the feeling aside, chalking it up the head injury. To distract himself he watched a police officer take statements from the bystanders, while the paramedics bustled around.

Breathing deeply to stay his rising panic, Aidan looked towards the collection of his neighbors. He wished they would all go home instead of gawking. Maybe real life suffering was more entertaining than the fabricated stuff on TV. He scanned the faces of the crowd, taking stock of all the usual busybodies.

There was old Mrs. Eizer, the local cat lady. Beside her, stood Mr. Beinger, and his gossiping wife. It was the usual cast who pretended to be perfect while pointing out the faults of their neighbors. Aidan felt a particular surge of fury as he recognized the man from the window standing slightly apart from the group.

The man stared at him blatantly, unabashed when Aidan met his gaze, and scowled. In the darkness, and at such a distance it was difficult to make out his features clearly, but Aidan guessed he was in his late thirties. He had dark hair, which was short, and tidy under his tilted fedora. He was dressed neatly, his trench coat open, and hands in his suit pant pockets. He was out of place on the suburban street, but no one else seemed to notice him.

Aidan turned away angrily, and watched one of the ambulances speed down the street. They were in a rush to get someone to the hospital. His throat constricted as he thought of his mother. Had she been seriously hurt? Guilt made his shoulder stiffen. Why hadn't he thought of her sooner?

He jogged to the other ambulance, and breathed a sigh of relief as he saw his mother sitting on a gurney while a paramedic attended to her. Tears streamed down her cheeks, and he wanted to comfort her, but he kept his distance so the paramedic could work. Neither of them took any notice of him.

"How is my son?" Sarah stammered.

"Ma'am, let me attend to your injuries." The paramedic insisted gently, stabilizing her arm. "You will be able to see him soon. Try to relax." He said as he helped her lay back on the gurney. With the help of another paramedic, they lifted her into the ambulance.

"Wait for me!" Aidan called, as he climbed into the back of the ambulance before the paramedic closed the back door. He settled himself into the corner to stay out of their way.

He leaned back, letting his head be cradled by the corner into which he was nestled. Aidan rubbed his face, and breathed deeply, calmer now that they were away from the house. Maybe everything would be okay now. Maybe this time, things would change.

Three...

"One should not stand at the foot of a sick person's bed, because that place is reserved for the guardian angel."
– Jewish proverb

As he followed the paramedics and his mother into the hospital, Aidan's first thought was that the waiting room seemed more crowded than usual. The second was that the hospital's usual sterile smell was missing. Instead, the air seemed sharp as if he was breathing in some invisible gas. He coughed, trying to clear his lungs of the uncomfortable stinging.

Each breath brought a stab of pain in his chest, forcing him to take shallow breaths. Aidan stopped, leaning on the wall for support as he struggled to take in air. He rubbed his chest, trying to ease the pain wracking his lungs. What the hell was happening? Was seventeen too young for a heart attack? He watched the paramedics take his mother into another room, but remained rooted in place by the pain.

He was about to signal for a nurse when he noticed a familiar face in the waiting area. The man's features, and grim expression stood out among the sea of faces. Aidan scowled, and looked away from the strange man. Like he didn't have enough problems already.

His shoulder pressed against the wall as he continued to fight off the effects of the burning air. He looked around the room, looking for signs of others experiencing the same symptoms. The other patients nursed their individual ailments, but none seemed to suffer from the same crippling pain he was experiencing.

Aidan frowned as he noticed the man coming towards him. He wrapped his arms tightly around his chest, trying to mask his pain as the stranger leaned on the wall a few feet down from him. Pretending to be preoccupied, Aidan stared across the waiting room, watching the man in his peripheral vision.

Gradually, breathing became easier as the pain subsided. He inhaled deeply, thankful that the attack had passed. Not daring to test his luck, he remained against the wall for a while longer. Glancing over, Aidan watched as the man drew out a prepared cigarette, and lit it. In the better light of the hospital, Aidan could see he was younger than he had first guessed, perhaps in his early thirties. Despite his youth, his expression was hard.

Aidan frowned, and looked around. No one else seemed to have noticed that the man was smoking. "This is a hospital. You shouldn't be smoking in here."

The stranger chuckled lowly, and shrugged, exhaling a cloud of smoke into the air. Aidan shivered at the man's laugh, unnerved by the sound's malice. "Put it out, or I'm calling the nurse." He said, trying not to sound petulant. The man's indifferent attitude made him feel like an annoying child.

"It won't do much good." The man muttered, with the cigarette still caught between his teeth. Red embers flared as he sucked in a lungful of smoke.

"Excuse me." Aidan said to one of the nurses as she passed by. She did not respond; her attention fixed on the chart she was reading as she walked. Aidan pushed away from the wall, and took a few quick steps to catch up to her. "Excuse me." He repeated, reaching out to touch her shoulder. His hand did not make contact however, as she dissolved from his grip. Aidan stumbled back, letting out a shout of surprise.

Behind him, the man snorted, exhaling clouds of smoke in short bursts.

"I tried to warn you, kid." He said as he tapped the ash off the end of his cigarette. The ash vanished as it floated down toward the ground.

"Who are you?" Aidan demanded as he turned back towards the man, keeping a cautious distance between them. "What's going on?"

"Name's Asmodeus." The man answered. He took another drag of his cigarette, and then flicked it across the floor. Pulling away from the wall, he straightened his coat, and walked towards the elevator. "Come on." He beckoned without turning back.

Aidan held his ground, watching Asmodeus. He had no intention of following him.

As he reached the elevator, Asmodeus glanced back at him, a smirk on his lips. "You will feel better if you stay with me." He commented lazily. He grunted when Aidan remained in place. "Suit yourself."

As the distance between him, and Asmodeus grew, the chest pain started to overtake Aidan again. Stubbornly Aidan stayed where he was. He wanted nothing to do with this man. His choice in the matter was removed however, as breathing became more painful. He realized that no one else was even aware of him, never mind in a position to help. Cursing bitterly under his breath, he stumbled after Asmodeus.

"Wait. Aren't you going to tell me what's happening?" Aidan gasped as he pursued him. He noticed immediately that the pain lessened as he drew closer to the stranger.

"It'll be easier to show you. Hurry up; I don't have all night." Asmodeus chuckled darkly, enjoying the irony of his last statement. Time was one thing he had in abundance.

Hesitantly Aidan obeyed, the pain subsiding entirely as he trailed a few steps behind Asmodeus.

≈≈≈≈≈≈≈≈≈

Aidan stood beside a hospital bed, staring down at the motionless body lying there. Asmodeus stood at the end of the bed, barely concealing his impatience as Aidan took his time studying the features of the boy in the bed. It took him even longer to acknowledge that they were his own features.

"How…how is this possible?" Aidan whispered, struggling to form the words. He ran his fingers over the fabric of the jeans he wore, confirming that they still felt real to him. "What happened to me?"

"You fell, and hit your head," Asmodeus said blandly, not offering sympathy or a further explanation.

Memories flooded back to Aidan in a flash. He recalled the impact of Tyler's fist, and his mother screaming. He could even recall the sensation of falling, and the feel of the coffee table against his temple, but not the pain that should have accompanied it.

"Am I dead?" He felt foolish asking, but the shock had numbed him.

Asmodeus nodded towards the heart monitor by the bed. A steady beep filled the room, tracking the pace of his heart. "Not according to that thing. The doctors mentioned a coma."

Aidan looked back at the body lying on the bed. Nervously he reached out, and touched his own hand. His hand remained solid under his touch, unlike the nurse earlier. So much for the Hollywood concept that he could lay down, and sink back into his body.

"So, are you an angel?" Aidan could hear the doubt in his own voice. He had never considered himself religious, but this was not how he would have imagined an angel. This man seemed so jaded, and uncaring.

"Close enough," Asmodeus muttered, rolling a cigarette between his fingertips. He let his attention focus on the task of preparing the cigarette, doing his best to ignore the boy.

"How do I go back?" He looked back towards Asmodeus. He was desperate for help, even if it was from this miserable man.

"That's the first good question you've asked, kid," Asmodeus responded sharply. He scowled at Aidan, unable to contain his irritation.

Aidan glared back at him. "You don't know either, do you?"

"No, but I'll be glad to find out if it means an end to your questions." He quipped.

"Let's go then," Aidan said quickly, sharing the sentiment of being free of Asmodeus as quickly as possible.

"*We* are not going anywhere." Asmodeus said, emphasizing the first word. "I am going alone."

"So I'm supposed to just wait here?" Aidan said.

Asmodeus shook his head. "You aren't staying here alone. I can't be sure you won't wander off." Putting his hand on Aidan's shoulder. Aidan flinched under his tight grip, never quite comfortable with physical contact.

"Close your eyes, and stop fidgeting," Asmodeus growled.

Aidan obeyed, and felt a surge of disorienting vertigo followed by a tugging feeling all over his body. Then the pressure of Asmodeus' grip was released.

"Open your eyes," He instructed.

Aidan opened his eyes to find himself standing in the middle of his living room. Everything was as they had left it. It was as if nothing in his life had changed.

"How did you do that?"

"Do you always ask so many questions, kid?" Asmodeus muttered, adjusting the tilt of his hat in the reflection of the window.

"My name is Aidan, not kid." He said, slowly sitting on the love seat. "And no, I usually don't, but I'm making an exception given the circumstances."

Asmodeus flicked a hand dismissively in his direction. "Sure, kid. Wait for me here. I have some business to take care of."

"When do I get some answers?" Aidan demanded, but Asmodeus was already gone.

Four...

"Woe to him that claims obedience when it is not due;
Woe to him that refuses it when it is."
– Thomas Carlyle

Asmodeus stared up at the bell tower of the cathedral across the street. Looking down, he dug out some paper from his pocket. Slowly he rolled some tobacco into the paper. It was a minor distraction, but it delayed facing Gabrielle's patronizing tone. Licking the paper, he sealed it, and tucked the cigarette behind his ear. Time to get it over with, he thought bitterly.

Crossing the street, Asmodeus ascended the steps, and entered the cathedral. Despite the stonewalls surrounding him, the air felt warm and smelled pure. A few humans sat dispersed in the pews, lost in their late night prayers, and succumbing to the calm surroundings.

Ignoring them, Asmodeus made his way towards where Zacharias stood guard at the bell tower staircase. As usual, Zacharias was dressed in a tan robe, which seemed better suited for centuries ago. His greying hair and beard was trimmed to perfection.

"Fashionable as always, Zach," Asmodeus said, with a hint of a smirk. He paused for a moment, lingering beside Zacharias.

"Asmodeus," Zacharias said tersely, failing to keep the irritation out of the greeting. "Gabrielle has been waiting for a report."

"She in a good mood?"

"Yes," Zacharias said hesitantly, knowing Asmodeus could sense Gabrielle's mood as clearly as he could.

"Let me ruin it," Asmodeus said with a smug smirk, which betrayed his dark humor.

Asmodeus started up the spiraling staircase of the bell tower. The calm atmosphere worked to soothe his bitter mood, but he combated the serene influence with his irritable temperament. He would not let Gabrielle get to him so easily. Reaching the top of the staircase, he glanced around the familiar surroundings.

The circular room was littered with support beams that held the three large bells aloft. The three bells differed in sizes, providing different tones to the melody they created. Large windows stretched as high as the bells, allowing their sound to carry freely out to the city.

Gabrielle stood at one of the many windows, watching the city below. The moonlight, which shone through the glassless window, lent a silver sheen to her gossamer dress. Her dark hair fell in waves down her back, covering what skin the dress exposed. Sensing his approach through the maze of beams, she looked over her shoulder.

"I was expecting a report at sunset." She said as she turned towards him. Despite her critical words, her tone was light. Gabrielle smiled warmly, undeterred by his determination to be in a foul mood.

"I was delayed." He said, reaching for his cigarette and then pulling out his lighter.

"Clearly," Gabrielle answered, eying the cigarette disapprovingly while trying not to give him the enjoyment of irritating her. "Is that truly necessary?" She asked, indicating the cigarette with a slight nod.

"Yea." A smirk tugged at the corner of his lips, suspecting that her good humor was wavering. "It makes me feel more human," Asmodeus muttered as he slipped the cigarette between his lips and lit it.

"You are far from human anymore." She pointed out. "It may have been fashionable during your time, but it is such a distasteful habit."

He shrugged, and tilted his head back, exhaling a thick stream of smoke into the air. Looking back towards Gabrielle, he noted with pleasure that her earlier smile had vanished.

"The report, Asmodeus." She said shortly, turning her back to him, and watching the dark street below. The temperature dropped a few degrees as a cool wind swept through the windows, and dispelled the pleasant warmth.

"Do you want the good news first?" Asmodeus caught the feel of her impatience and resisted the urge to laugh.

Gabrielle glanced towards him with a cool expression. "You are wasting my time, Asmodeus. That does not bode well for you." She said, and then turned back to the window, leaning against the ledge with both hands on the stone.

He removed the cigarette from his lips, and held it between his thumb and index finger. "Well, there's no good news." Asmodeus watched the embers burn at the end of his cigarette. "The kid's in a coma, and now he's trapped in our realm."

The only sound for a second was the rustle of the wind. All traces of Gabrielle's mood vanished from his perception, causing Asmodeus to arch an eyebrow curiously. She was rarely so evasive. Keeping his intrigue in check, he waited for her to speak.

"His prognosis?" Gabrielle asked, while keeping her back to him.

"The human doctors aren't sure. Lucky for you, his heart is still ticking for now." Asmodeus tossed the cigarette down, and crushed it under his shoe. "You don't seem upset that I let him get hurt."

"Did you allow him to be hurt purposely?" Gabrielle countered, glancing over her shoulder.

"No. You'll be glad to hear that I was following your orders."

"Remarkable." Gabrielle retorted dryly, facing him again, and approaching slowly. "Is he in a safe location?"

"I left him at the hospital with his body." He responded sarcastically, irritated by Gabrielle's questions.

"You left him in the Shades playground?" The temperature dropped sharply as Gabrielle glared at him accusingly.

"I'm not ignorant, Gabrielle," Asmodeus growled, feeling his own temper flare at her accusation. "The damn demons won't find him. I took him back to his house. Why is he so important?"

"He is to play an important role in our fight against the Shades."

"So a new pet then?" He replied mockingly, before asking a more serious question. "Is that why you assigned me as his chaperone?" Gabrielle's orders to protect Aidan made more sense now, although he still could not see what Gabrielle saw in the kid.

Ignoring his question, Gabrielle continued. "I have new orders for you. You will continue to guard Aidan, and in addition, you will begin training him." Asmodeus started to speak, but Gabrielle cut him off with a warning look. "If the Shades discover his importance to me, they will try to destroy his soul. I need him prepared to defend himself, in the event you fail again."

Asmodeus frowned at the quip at his competence, but let it pass. "Wouldn't Azriel be better suited to train the kid?"

"Azriel will spend some time tutoring him in some areas of our realm. However, I want the focus of his training to be spent with you in combat."

"Why him? He's a child." Asmodeus protested. "He is too young to suit the demands of being a fighter. The Shades will laugh and then tear him apart."

"I have never known you to be the sentimental type. Is his youth really your concern?" Gabrielle asked, sounding bemused.

"No, I was practicing being nice. Terribly out of character, I know." He admitted with a fiendish smirk. "But if I am being forced to train someone, I would prefer someone who is stronger and more worthwhile. I will be wasting my time with a child."

"His worth will not be determined by you. Nor are you a proper judge." Her tone was harsh as she rebuked him.

"Isn't there someone else who can babysit him?" Asmodeus complained, digging into his pocket for another cigarette. Pulling one out, he grimly thought about being stuck with the kid. He brought the cigarette to his lips, dismayed by the prospect of the child being his new companion. He must have irritated Gabrielle more than he was aware.

Gabrielle narrowed her eyes, and the cigarette burst into flames, disintegrating in his hand. "This is an order you will not disobey, Asmodeus. Aidan has value to me, and you will be satisfied with that knowledge."

Asmodeus grunted to acknowledge the command, still not pleased with his new orders. "Why now? You haven't trained a new hunter since you found me."

"Do not make the mistake of being arrogant. I have gone longer spans of time without training hunters. One hundred years is a short time in our history, and there have been other apprentices since you. You are not privy to all my decisions, however entitled you may feel." She informed him. "The Shades are gaining power quickly as the humans wage war. We need more hunters to be able to take back control. The Aduro cannot fall."

Pretending to be humbled, Asmodeus remained silent for a time. He pulled the tip of his hat over his eyes, glancing at her from under the brim. His jaw worked furiously, while grinding his teeth.

"And what of his human life? Do you expect him to abandon any hope of returning home?" He was softer in his questioning now.

"Now you are beginning to sound like Azriel. Are you certain you have not exchanged places?" She chuckled, looking at Asmodeus appraisingly. He gave her a withering glare. "I suppose not."

"How long do you expect the boy to be with us?" He said, keeping his voice controlled.

"Until he can fulfil the task that is his. I suggest you train him quickly, and thoroughly." Gabrielle said, smoothing the fabric of her dress. "I will be unable to return him to the human realm until the task is complete. There is an unknown force blocking my connection to the human realm."

"And what is this grand purpose he is destined for?"

"He will receive his orders directly from me when I feel his training is sufficient for the task. Do not concern yourself with the particulars."

Asmodeus grumbled but decided it was not worth further argument. "Anything else?"

"Do you understand your orders?" She looked towards him critically. Asmodeus nodded sharply, touching the brim of his hat in a half-hearted salute.

"Good, then you are dismissed."

Five...

"No generous mind delights to oppress the weak,
but rather to cherish and protect."
- Anne Bronte

Aidan sat on his bed, listening to Jeopardy playing in the next room. The TV had been left on in all the chaos. He tapped his foot on the floor, unsettled by the emptiness of the house. Getting up, he paced his room and let his thoughts wander. As much as he tried to reassure himself, he could not shake the feeling of dread.

His thoughts consistently turned back to his Mom. Had she been given the news about his coma yet? He could imagine how worried she would be. What about Jazmine? What would she think when he didn't show up at school? Allowing himself some hope, he wondered if this could all be a dream. It all felt surreal enough to be one.

Desperate to pass the time, he wandered the house looking for a distraction. He found himself in the kitchen, absentmindedly watching the seconds tick by on the clock above the doorway. As the minutes passed, he became more impatient with waiting for Asmodeus to return.

Closing his eyes, he tried to find a way to replicate the tug he had felt with Asmodeus. When he opened his eyes, he was disappointed to find himself still standing in the kitchen. Walking to the front door, he reached for the handle, but his hand passed through the knob. Cringing, he squeezed his eyes shut and stepped forward.

He ignored the strange sensation that ran through him as he passed through the door. Only once the feeling stopped did he slowly open his eyes to find himself on the front steps. Aidan let out a relieved breath, pleased with his success. Without hesitating, he set off for the hospital. Thankfully, they didn't live very far away. He guessed it would take him about an hour to walk there. However, he discovered that he reached the hospital much faster than he had expected. Distance seemed to matter less.

When he crossed the threshold of the hospital doors, the air began to burn his lungs as it had before. As he ventured farther into the hospital, the pain began to seep into the rest of his body, slowing his progress. Doing his best to ignore the pain, he followed the route to his room.

Arriving at his room, he stared at his motionless body. Beside the bed, his mother, Sarah, sat in a metal chair. She held his hand in hers, her other arm in a cast. Tears rolled down her cheeks, but she didn't bother to brush them away.

Behind his mother, a black haired woman stood with her hand on Sarah's shoulder. The woman appeared young, perhaps in her forties. The woman whispered in Sarah's ear, but Sarah didn't respond to the woman's voice. Instead, Sarah only sobbed harder, growing more distraught by the second. Whatever the woman was saying was doing nothing to comfort his Mother.

"Mom," Aidan said, going to her side, and placed his hand over hers. He ignored the dark-haired woman entirely, expecting that she couldn't see him. "Everything will be okay. Don't cry." He murmured, wishing desperately that he could comfort her.

The dark-haired woman turned towards him sharply, her lips curling into a possessive sneer. "She's mine. Back off!"

Aidan leapt back, startled by the woman's reaction. "You can see me?"

The woman smirked. "Ah, a freshie." Letting go of Sarah, she moved towards Aidan, watching him with a predatory glint in her eye. "Question is, are you an Aduro or a Shade?" She mused to herself, continuing to look him over appraisingly.

"What?" Aidan said, maneuvering himself to stand between the woman and his mother. Once there, he held his ground with a determined glare.

"No matter. You won't be around much longer." The woman said, her intentions no longer on his mother.

Aidan blinked, and suddenly the woman was in front of him, her grip tightened around his throat. He struggled in her grip, but he could not break her hold. As hard as he tried, he couldn't tear his gaze away from her cruel eyes. He could feel her presence creeping into his mind like a cold chill. His struggles weakened as he felt his energy begin to fade. The woman's grin broadened, his energy making her stronger.

Out of the corner of his eye, Aidan noticed a shadowy figure watching the struggle. He tried to call out for help, but his voice wouldn't work.

Hearing his Mom cry, Aidan felt his anger rise. He wouldn't leave her, not without a fight at least. The heat of his fury began to push away the chill of the woman's control. With a yell, he broke the woman's grasp of his mind and throat. Staggering back, he fell onto the cold tile of the floor.

The woman stumbled back a few steps as well, and looked surprised by his outburst of rage. "Not bad, little one. You should be a Shade." She said, as she straightened up. She was barely fazed by the assault, while Aidan was panting in exhaustion.

Focusing on his fury, Aidan got to his feet. "Leave!" He said threateningly.

"Tsk. Tsk freshie. Get out of here before I get angry." She scolded, reaching out to Sarah again.

Feeling more self-assured, Aidan snatched her wrist, and pulled her hand away from his Mom. "I said leave." He said more forcefully.

Learning from her example, he instinctively reached out for her mind. As he touched her consciousness, his mind was submerged in overwhelming darkness. Instead of gaining strength from her, he could feel the ebb of his own strength again. Unable to release her physically, and mentally, his knees gave out from under him, and he looked up at her.

She leaned forward, running her finger along his cheek. "Now you'll learn never to interrupt a Shades work. Not that you'll ever get the chance again." She gloated.

The woman smirked at him. Her lips moved again, but he could not hear her words. Desperately he tried to cling to his anger to fend her off again. His efforts only seemed to feed her more, now that she was prepared. Malice glinted in her eyes, as she grabbed hold of his wrist. She had to hold Aidan up as he was weakened enough that he struggled to keep his balance.

He was certain that she would consume his mind entirely, he felt her concentration waver, and his mind was released. Her fear became tangible to him. Vaguely he wondered if he should be afraid too, but was too weak to feel anything, but vague concern.

"Leave him!" Asmodeus commanded sharply.

The woman released Aidan instantly, and he fell back again, struggling for consciousness. He moved his head, looking towards where Asmodeus towered in the doorway. Relief replaced some of his exhaustion. He thought to warn Asmodeus about the woman, but his voice was barely a whisper.

Gaining some of her nerve back, the woman narrowed her eyes. "They are mine. I claim them!" She hissed.

Before the woman could move, Asmodeus crossed the room, and grabbed hold of her throat. He lifted her off the ground to match his eye level. "Wrong choice." He said in a silky voice.

"You're an Aduro...?" She gasped her expression now a mixture of confusion and terror.

He laughed darkly and grinned widely at her. "Worse, darling. I'm Asmodeus." He said, pleased when the widening of her eyes seemed to indicate that she recognized his name. "But you won't have a chance to make the mistake twice." He gave a crooked grin as his grip tightened on her neck.

He locked his gaze with hers, and she froze, unable to move. Her eyes began to dim as a dark mist seeped from her, and crossed the distance between them, and was absorbed into Asmodeus. Within seconds the woman had dissolved completely and vanished. Moving to Aidan's side, Asmodeus glared down at him.

"I told you to wait at the house, idiot!" Asmodeus seethed. "You can't even protect yourself from a damn scavenger." He complained, thinking of Gabrielle's orders.

Aidan struggled back to his feet, and leaned on the wall for support. "My Mom..." He muttered, looking over to where Sarah sat shaking with fear.

Asmodeus glanced towards her, and gave an annoyed sigh. Suddenly, his demeanor shifted drastically and his harsh gaze softened. His sudden calm soothed the anger out of the room and relaxed Sarah. "She's fine. Humans are sensitive to our emotions." He said in a kinder voice.

Aidan nodded, not fully comprehending what Asmodeus meant. His eyes slipped closed, and he felt himself lose balance, unable to fight the overwhelming weakness any longer. The last thing he was aware of was

being caught in steady arms, before all sensation
vanished.

Six...

"Though it be honest, it is never good to bring bad news."
– William Shakespeare

The halls of the high school buzzed with activity as students shared their weekend gossip and a mess of lanky bodies became a maze to weave through on the way to lockers and classrooms. Jazz navigated the chaos as quickly as possible, trying to avoid anyone she might know. Early morning chatter only served to annoy her, and the excitement made her irritable first thing in the day. A slow start had always been her preference, but high school didn't fit that agenda well.

Reaching her locker, Jazz sorted through the jumble of books to find the one she would need for the first period. Tucking the book into her bag, she glanced around for Aidan. It was out of character for him to not be waiting for her. He was usually one of the first to arrive at the school.

For the first time, she noticed the peculiar looks she was receiving from the students clustered nearby. Glancing into the mirror, she looked for the reason for the whispered conversation. Finding nothing out of the ordinary, she closed the locker. Slinging her bag over her shoulder, she walked to where she spent lunch breaks with Aidan every day.

Only as she walked down the halls, did she notice that the usual Monday morning chatter was more subdued than normal. In fact, the gossiping voices seemed to lack the usual excitement. Frowning, Jazz took a seat at her usual bench, trying to ignore the less than subtle glances in her direction.

Despite her growing apprehension, Jazz nodded a greeting as Kirsten approached her. Her welcoming expression faded into uncertainty as she noticed the other girl's sympathetic look. "Hey, Kirsten, what's up?" Jazz said, trying to remember the last time they had talked. They had shared a few classes together, and some friendly conversations, but they were more acquaintances than friends.

"Hey, Jazz. How are you doing?" Kirsten said, not hiding the concern in her voice.

"I'm fine." Jazz responded hesitantly, bemused by her classmate's behavior. "How about you?"

"I'm good." She said, sitting beside Jazz.

Kirsten gave her a forced smile, making Jazz wonder if there was something she knew. She began to feel more uneasy.

"Listen, if there's anything I can do for you. Let me know, okay? Things will probably be okay but-." Kirsten said, feeling awkward, and unsure about what to say.

Jazz frowned and cut her off. "What are you talking about?"

"About Aidan," Kirsten said, her concern shifting to embarrassment.

"What about him?"

"You don't know?" Kirsten said, looking horrified that she had to be the one to deliver the news.

"Know what?" Jazmin asked. Horrible scenarios started jumping to mind as she watched Kirsten's reaction. Panic made her heart flutter, and she clutched her bag closer.

Had Aidan been in an accident? Was he hurt? Or maybe he was cheating, and she was the last to know? But Aidan wouldn't do that to her. He loved her. Even if he hadn't said it, his actions spoke for him. At least that was what she had been telling herself.

"It was on the news this morning," Kirsten said, easing into the news. "The police were called to his house last night. They didn't say his name, but it's pretty obvious. The news said he was taken to the hospital and is in a coma. His Dad was arrested. I thought you knew…" She spoke in a flurry.

"No. I had no idea." Jazz said, barely able to speak. She said, frozen in place by the news. Finally, she broke free of her shock, and stood quickly. "I have to go. Thanks for telling me."

"Wait. Where are you going?" Kirsten called after her, but Jazz didn't respond.

She moved through the hallways in a daze. The other students moved out of her way, giving her curious looks. Now she understood the change in the school.

Reaching the bus stop, Jazz sat down heavily. She focused on keeping her breathing slow and steady so she wouldn't panic. There was no sense in panicking…yet.

≈≈≈≈≈≈≈≈

The smell of the hospital churned her stomach as usual, but Jazmine disregarded the unsettling feeling. Now was not the time to let her hospital anxiety stop her. Walking resolutely to the nurse's station, Jazmine made a point to ignore the shadows moving at the edge of her vision.

Hearing her approach, the nurse looked up from her paperwork. "How can I help you?"

"Aidan Matheson's room, please."

Nodding, the nurse typed his name into the computer. "Room 314 in the south tower. Do you need directions?"

Not wanting to waste time she nodded. The nurse nodded, and pointed towards one of the wings. "Down that way. Take the first set of elevators up. Follow the signage."

"Thanks," Jazmine answered, and set off in the direction the nurse had indicated. Impatiently, she waited for the elevator. As the doors closed, and the machine jerked into action, her stomach lurched uncomfortably. The sensation did not help the nervous twisting of her stomach. All kinds of scenarios whirled in her mind. What if Aidan never woke up?

Trying to settle her rampant thoughts, Jazz stepped out of the elevator, and gathered her bearings. A deep, steadying breath calmed her jitters as shadows flitted around in the peripheral of her vision. She tried to keep her gaze from darting around to follow the movement. Instead, she stared directly ahead, determined to ignore the shadows which had haunted her since childhood.

As an imaginative child, her parents had attributed her descriptions of strange new friends as imaginary characters. She could describe all her imaginary friends in elaborate detail, and explain their different personalities. Her parents had accepted her imagination with good humor, at least until the day of her grandmother's funeral.

As an outgoing eight-year-old, Jazz hadn't understood everyone's grief at her grandma's funeral. Trying to ease the pain of those at the funeral reception, she had started delivering the messages that her grandmother had whispered to her. Instead of providing comfort, her messages only served to upset everyone.

Jazz could still vividly recall how upset her Mother had been. As her Mom sobbed, her Father tried to explain to her that it was time for her to stop imagining things, and that her grandmother was gone. It only took one look at her distraught Mother for Jazz to decide he was right.

Since then she had vowed to ignore any strange occurrences, and never upset anyone again. Jazz was careful not to speak of the strange things she saw. Gradually, her sightings became less and less as she vehemently ignored what she had once acknowledged. Now, only the shadows lurking in hospital hallways, and graveyards threatened to shatter her illusion of normalcy.

Following the trail of hospital signs, Jazz looked for room 314. As she finally found the room, Jazz hesitated for a moment. Taking a deep breath to steady her nerves, she then entered the room.

She stopped abruptly in the threshold of the door, unprepared for the sight that greeted her. Machines lined the wall behind Aidan's bed, monitoring his various vital signs. Despite the machinery, he appeared to be sleeping. Moving to his side, Jazz touched his hand timidly. "Oh, Aidan." She whispered, perching herself on the edge of the bed. His stillness was the most unnerving part.

She touched his face, tracing his familiar features. A large welt and dark bruise had spread across his temple. She ran her fingers through his dark hair, watching his peaceful expression for any sign of awareness. Jazz let out a long slow breath, missing the deep green of his eyes.

"Why didn't you tell me?" Jazz whispered, starting to feel foolish as she talked to him with no hope of a response. She continued to watch him intently, wishing he would wake up. She exhaled roughly, and then perched on the side of his bed, while continuing to hold his hand.

All the sounds of the hospital faded into the background as she focused all her attention on him. She searched desperately for some sign that he was aware. Her focus on him remained so complete that she didn't hear the footsteps of someone's arrival in the room.

"Excuse me, who are you?" A woman's voice said suspiciously, a sharp edge to her tone.

Jazz jumped, startled by the intrusion. She turned and looked towards the woman standing in the doorway. The woman seemed exhausted, and her eyes were swollen from crying. Glancing between the woman and Aidan, Jazz noticed the resemblance immediately. She stood quickly, releasing Aidan's hand and feeling awkward.

"I'm Jazmine. Aidan's girlfriend. Most people call me Jazz, though." Jazz said in a rush. "You must be Mrs. Matheson."

Sarah nodded, and went to the chair beside the bed, sinking into it. "Aidan talked about you, so I should have known. I'm sorry if I was rude." She said as she looked towards her motionless son.

"It's okay." Jazz responded, somewhat surprised that Sarah knew about her. She hesitated awkwardly, and then slowly sat on the edge of the bed again. "I wish we could have met under better circumstances."

"Me too. It's a shame Aidan never invited you over."

Jazz nodded in agreement, but was eager to change the topic. Glancing at the cast on Sarah's arm, she frowned a bit. "How is your arm?"

"I'll be fine. Nothing that time won't mend." Sarah said with optimism that wasn't convincing. She glanced at Aidan, her forehead creasing with concern. It wasn't too hard to guess that she was contemplating whether time would mend her son as well.

Guessing her thoughts, Jazz looked towards Aidan as well. "Have the doctors said anything about his recovery?"

"They ran a CT scan last night, and a SPECT scan this morning. All they know is that it is a coma induced by head trauma. At least that's all that they have told me." Sarah paused for a moment to take a shaky breath.

"The doctor said that he would run another test today. The tests will give us some idea about his chances of recovery." Her voice thickened with emotion as she spoke.

Jazz nodded a bit, and looked away from Sarah. It always felt awkward to watch adults cry. Slipping her hand under Aidan's, she laced her fingers between his tightly. She blinked rapidly, trying to maintain her composure.

"Is it okay if I stay for a bit?" Jazz asked after sitting in silence for a while.

"Of course, dear. I'm sure he would like that." Sarah said, her voice still rough with emotion. "The doctor did mention it is helpful for him to hear familiar voices."

Jazz nodded again, stroking Aidan's hand. "What happened?"

Sarah tensed, her expression becoming anxious as she recalled the previous night's events. Immediately, Jazz regretted the question.

"Forget I asked. It isn't any of my business." Jazz said.

Sarah seemed relieved not to have to verbalize the incident, and regained her composure. "It's fine." She leaned back in her chair, her posture heavy with exhaustion.

Jazz sat for a while, and then pulled some paper from her pocket. She fished out a pen, and then wrote down her number. "If you need anything, call me anytime." She said, holding the paper out to Sarah.

Sarah took the paper. "Thank you. I should be okay."

"I know." Jazz said gently. "But just in case."

"Thanks," Sarah said, managing a small smile. "I appreciate it."

"It's nothing." Jazz said.

Then they lapsed into a less awkward silence, the steady sounds of machines filling the void of conversation.

Seven...

"She looked at him, as one who awakes:
The past was a sleep and her life began."
– Robert Browning

Aidan was roused by the sound of birds chirping outside a nearby window. He groaned weakly, his limbs feeling heavy and listless. Memories of the fight at the hospital returned, and in a panic, he tried to gather energy to defend himself. With his eyes only half-opened, he started to roll onto his side to sit up, rebelling against his sluggish limbs.

"Easy there, son." A soothing voice cautioned him.

Aidan recognized Asmodeus's voice, but the gentle tone sounded foreign compared to his usually rough words. Aidan felt a hand rest on his shoulder, applying gentle pressure to keep him from sitting up. Gradually a calm feeling washed over him, carrying away all traces of his anxiety.

"You need to rest and recover," The man said, as he moved across the room, once he was sure Aidan wouldn't attempt getting up again. "You have strained yourself, and need to regain your lost energy."

Aidan forced his eyes open, and squinted to focus his vision. He squinted around the room, trying to gather his bearings. He blinked a few times, still trying to clear his vision. Sunlight streamed in through the bay window across from the couch. The sitting room was furnished sparsely with dark wood and aged furniture. Underneath him, he could feel the cool leather of the sofa. Across the room, Asmodeus stood at a cabinet, pouring liquid from a decanter into a glass.

"Asmodeus? What happened?" Aidan said.

His caretaker turned towards him. His usual cynical expression was replaced with a more genuine interest. "You have confused me with another. My name is Azriel."

"But you said your name was Asmodeus at the hospital," Aidan said, perplexed by the man he was certain he had met before; unless Asmodeus had a kinder twin.

"Your confusion is understandable," Azriel said, sitting in an armchair beside the sofa. "It is a complicated existence, but essentially we are two souls occupying the same form."

Aidan stared blankly at Azriel, taking a few seconds to decipher what he had said. His thoughts still felt muddled and slow. "How is that possible?" Aidan said, uncertain if he was being sincere.

"That is a long story, and one which is better suited for another time," Azriel said. "Although Asmodeus and I are the same in appearance, we are very different. As I'm sure you have noticed, he is rather blunt and short-tempered. However, he will not harm you, so you need not fear him. That being said, I suggest you do not anger him."

Aidan nodded slowly, still struggling to comprehend what Azriel was saying. He felt as if he was wading through mental quicksand. "So you're like a split personality or something?"

Azriel's grin broadened, genuinely amused by the notion. "That is an adequate description."

"So, do you share memories too?"

"Asmodeus and I can share what we wish the other to know. Try not to think of us as one being, Aidan, but rather, as two." Azriel said. Gently, he helped Aidan sit up. "Drink this; it will help." Azriel placed the glass in the boy's hand and rose from his chair. Moving across the room, he hung the fedora and trench coat on the coat stand.

As Aidan watched, he began to notice distinct differences between how Azriel carried himself compared to Asmodeus. Azriel had a relaxed demeanor, whereas Asmodeus had seemed impatient with everything. Asmodeus's permanent scowl had been replaced by a content expression. It did seem that despite the two occupying the same presence, Aidan was truly meeting another individual.

Suspiciously, Aidan looked down into the glass. The liquid was a deep blue that shimmered silver as the light touched the surface. He sniffed experimentally at the drink, and found it had a sweet scent that reminded him of lavender.

"What is this?" He said, looking towards Azriel.

"Humans require energy to survive, as do we. Humans eat food to nourish themselves, whereas we feed on emotion. The glass contains harvested emotion. It will replace the energy you lost in the fight." He explained.

Aidan hesitated, but decided to trust Azriel. He did feel weak as if he hadn't eaten in far too long. Bringing the glass to his lips, he took a wary sip. The drink was sweet like honey, and the taste was addictive. His small sip turned into a more enthusiastic gulp once he established it was to his liking.

As he drank, Aidan began to feel better. Now that his energy was returning, questions began to surface about everything that had happened. However, he didn't speak until he had drained the last of the drink, unable to resist the sweet flavor.

"What is this place, Azriel?" Aidan said as he set the glass aside.

"It is my home, or at least it was. The humans see it as a ruin, but to us, it is as I remember it." Azriel looked around the room fondly, clearly at ease in the surroundings.

"It is nice. But, I meant this whole place. Is it a dream?" He asked, hating how ignorant he felt.

Azriel laughed. "That is a very good question. Although one that will take some time to answer." He paused for a moment, assessing Aidan's condition. "How do you feel?"

"Much better. The drink helped." Aidan said gratefully. "But now I need answers."

Azriel nodded in agreement. "Then I will try to answer all of your questions." He returned to the armchair and sat. "Make yourself comfortable, and I will explain."

Aidan shifted his position on the couch so that they faced each other. Trying to be patient, he waited for Azriel to begin.

"First, this is no dream. Rather our existence is parallel to the human realm. As you have experienced, we can see them, but not touch them. For the most part, humans cannot see us; however, they are sensitive to our existence. Our two worlds are very much dependent on each other."

Azriel paused for a moment, considering his next words. He rested his elbows on the arms of the chair, and pressed his fingertips together. Aidan met the steel blue of his gaze, finding his expression much gentler than Asmodeus's had been.

"As I mentioned, we are dependent on the energy created by emotions. We thrive on the energy humans produce through their emotions." Azriel explained.

"It sounds like you need us more than we need you," Aidan commented, his tone harsher than he meant it to be.

"Do not forget Aidan; you currently exist in our world, which means you must live by the rules of our existence, or perish." Azriel reminded him gently. "The energy you, and I, absorb from the humans does not harm them. For example, when a human is happy, their emotions produce the energy we require to thrive. We do not deplete their happiness by taking this energy; rather their emotions are a catalyst for producing the energy."

Aidan frowned, thinking back to the woman who had been with his mother. "What about sadness, does that give off the same energy?"

Azriel nodded gravely. "Yes, there are some who prefer to feed off of emotions such as sadness or anger. Those souls are referred to as the Shades. Souls who feed off happiness, and other positive emotions are known as the Aduro or hunters."

"So are you angels and demons?" Aidan inquired.

"Not in the biblical sense, but it is a close enough comparison," Azriel responded wryly.

"There was a woman at the hospital. She said she was Shade." Aidan said, reflecting on what had happened.

"Yes, the hospital is a favorite location of the Shades. We do not simply feed off the energy produced by humans; we can also influence emotions, and events to some extent. Shades thrive off of the negative aspects of life, so they attempt to provoke fights, encourage illness, and pain."

Aidan frowned as he listened to Azriel. He began to feel irritated as he considered what Azriel was saying. "So are you saying that everything we feel is because of your kind?" He said indignantly, struggling to maintain an even tone.

Azriel's calm was not swayed by Aidan's irritation. "Of course not. Our attempts to influence emotions are only attempts. The freedom of choice is a human's greatest gift. We can create conditions for our desired outcome, but we cannot control a human's reaction. Can you ever recall a time when you lost your temper over something that shouldn't have angered you as much as it did?"

Aidan paused for a moment as he considered the question. He could think of numerous situations where he had been miserable without cause, and said things he shouldn't have. He thought of his father and his unexplainable mood swings. His sudden changes had seemed so irrational.

"You have likely experienced the influence of a Shade. However, whether you decided to act on that anger was your choice." Azriel said, carefully ignoring Aidan's guilty look after his explanation.

"There has been a constant struggle raging between the Shades and Aduros for centuries. The more suffering and negative emotions there are in the world, the stronger the Shades become. The Shades have been gaining an advantage for some time now, but we hope to slow their progress." Azriel paused for a moment, his expression grim. Then his pleasant expression returned, and he chuckled. "I apologize, I am getting carried away. Our war is not your concern."

"I assume you are an Aduro," Aidan asked, and was pleased when Azriel nodded. "Is Asmodeus a Shade?"

"I can understand your assumption. However, despite his rather bleak temperament, he stands with the Aduro. His anger is an effective weapon even against a Shade; he overwhelms them with his fury until they are destroyed."

Aidan felt himself shiver as he recalled Asmodeus's rage at the hospital, and how he had dealt with the Shade. He looked around the room to avoid Azriel's gaze. It was troubling to think that this man possessed two identities, which were so vastly different. He hoped he would only have to deal with Azriel, since Asmodeus reminded him too much of his Father.

Sitting in silence, Aidan tried to absorb everything Azriel had told him. The new world he found himself in, was overwhelming, but with Azriel's guidance, he found himself coping better than he would have expected. "So is this life after death that everyone is expecting?"

"That is one question which I cannot answer entirely. We don't understand why some souls linger here after leaving the human world, and why others continue beyond this realm. Even we do not know what is beyond this world." Azriel's brow furrowed, his expression becoming uncomfortable.

Aidan frowned as well. "You mean you can die here as well?"

"In a sense. We do not have physical bodies, but our souls still require energy to survive. If our souls are starved of energy or damaged too greatly, we will vanish. Where we go after this realm, is a mystery. Perhaps our souls are meant to forever travel through infinite realms of existence." Azriel said philosophically. "So even here, you must be careful if you wish to return to the human world."

Aidan nodded, as the gravity of the situation hit him. He was silent for a while as he let the news sink in. "So were you a human before this?" He asked.

"I was, although it has been a long time since I existed in the human realm. Nearly a hundred years."

Aidan arched a brow, surprised by Azriel's response. "So were you Azriel or Asmodeus as a human?"

"Neither in fact. As a human, we lived a different existence." Azriel admitted, his expression becoming bleak as bitter memories returned. "It took a series of events for our creation to occur." He fell silent after that, his pained expression indicating that the topic should be abandoned.

Avoiding Azriel's uncomfortable stare, Aidan quickly changed the topic with another question. "At the hospital, Asmodeus referred to the Shade as a scavenger. What did he mean?"

"A scavenger is one who strictly feeds off energy. For the most part, they are relatively harmless except against someone who is untrained in defense."

"She was feeding off my Mom. Will she be okay?"

Azriel nodded. "She will be fine. Most humans are upset enough while at the hospital that the Shades don't feel the need to upset them any further. They have enough sorrow, and pain to feed off without needing to create more."

Aidan looked down sadly, knowing that he was the cause of his Mother's pain. Not wanting to think about it, he tried to distract himself by continuing with his seemingly endless questions. "Why didn't Asmodeus help me when I was fighting the Shade?"

Azriel arched a brow slightly, surprised by his question. "He did, he saved you by stopping her from depleting your energy. If she had continued to drain you, you would have left this realm as well." Azriel responded.

"I know he stopped her, but he stood there and watched for a minute. It seemed like he was waiting for something. I didn't see his face, but it must have been him."

Azriel's expression became distant for a moment then he seemed to return his attention to Aidan. "He arrived, and wasted no time rescuing you. He would not risk your safety by delaying, so I can assure you it was not him whom you saw. Are you certain there wasn't another presence in the room?" Azriel asked, appearing troubled.

Aidan shrugged noncommittally. "I doubt it."

"Could you sense if it meant any harm?"

"I don't know. I only saw him for a moment before he vanished." Aidan tried to recall what had occurred at the hospital. His main recollection was the bewildering sensations that he had experienced. He frowned slightly as he recalled the pain when he had first arrived.

"Can I be influenced by the Shade?" Aidan asked. He quickly explained what he had felt at the hospital, and how the pain had vanished when he had been with Asmodeus.

Azriel couldn't help, but be impressed by Aidan's understanding. "Yes, their presence in such large numbers can make it painful for an untrained Aduro. However, while you are here, you are protected from their influence by my abilities. None the less, Gabrielle wishes you to be trained so you will be able to defend yourself."

"Gabrielle?" He asked, unfamiliar with the name.

"Gabrielle is one of the upper-level Aduro who oversees us. You will meet her once you have completed some of your training." Azriel explained.

Aidan shook his head as Azriel mentioned training. "I don't want any training; I want to go home. I don't belong here."

"You will need some training if you are to survive in our world."

"Can't you send me back?" Aidan demanded. With his curiosity about this new realm satisfied, he recalled his earlier desire to return to his Mother and Jazmine. He knew they would be worrying, and felt guilty for delaying as much as he had.

"Unfortunately, I am not that powerful. The only one powerful enough to do so is Gabrielle, and an unknown power is blocking even her ability. She has instructed me to train you before presenting you to her." He responded calmly, undeterred by Aidan's frustration.

"Not what I wanted to hear," Aidan grumbled angrily. Having no control over a situation made his temper flare quickly.

Azriel watched him, noticing his demeanor. "I think that's enough for now." He gave no reaction to Aidan's mood, seeming to have endless patience even as the boy grunted in reply. Standing, Azriel spoke once more. "You are welcome to explore the house as much as you like. You are protected within these walls and garden, so do not venture farther than the garden gate."

"Thanks," Aidan said, his tone not matching his polite reply.

"Rest well," said Azriel, and left him to contemplate all he had been told.

Eight...

*"Loyalty is a feature in a boy's character
that inspires boundless hope."*
- Sir Robert Baden-Powell

Jazz lay with her head resting on the edge of Aidan's bed, her hand still curled over his. Her thumb brushed over his hand, memorizing the feel of his skin. She longed for the sound of his voice, and the feel of his touch.

She tightened her grip on his hand, thinking about what he must have been through. Lifting her head, she looked towards where Sarah sat motionlessly. She was about to say something when she spotted the doctor standing in the doorway. Jazz straightened in her chair as Sarah rose to meet the doctor as he entered, greeting him with a weary smile.

"Hello, Doctor Briggs." Sarah motioned to Jazmine. "This is Jazmine."

Jazmine shook hands with the doctor.

"I have a few things I wanted to discuss with you, Mrs. Matheson." The doctor said to Sarah, glancing towards Jazmine before he continued.

Understanding his hesitation, Sarah spoke. "It is okay. I want Jazmine involved." She said. Jazmine felt a wave of gratitude for the woman, knowing she didn't have to allow her to stay. Satisfied, the doctor motioned for them to take a seat. Jazmine settled herself into the chair beside Sarah.

"With your permission, I would like to conduct a few tests to assess your son's prognosis for recovery." The doctor said as he pulled a chair over to sit with them.

"What kind of tests?" Sarah asked.

"It's called the Glasgow Coma Scale. It is designed to test his visual, verbal, and motor responses. A score of three to fifteen is assigned based on his responses. Fifteen is a normally functioning person, while three is a person in a coma." Doctor Briggs explained.

Jazz listened intently, wondering what exactly these tests entailed. The name of the test meant little to her. She glanced at Aidan, guessing that it would likely not have positive news. Aidan had not shown any sign of awareness in the time she had been here.

"Since you are his guardian, I'll need you to sign some consent forms for the tests." The doctor said, handing Sarah a clipboard.

Jazz watched as Sarah took the clipboard, and read through the paperwork. Once she had finished reading, she signed the pages, and then returned the clipboard to the doctor.

"Thank you. The tests will take some time. Why don't you both get something to eat? There's a cafeteria on the main floor. I should have the results by the time you return."

Sarah hesitated, unwilling to leave Aidan's side. Jazz touched her arm lightly. "I am a bit hungry. Will you come to get something to eat with me?" Jazz lied, forcing some lightness into her voice. Food wasn't appealing at all, but she suspected Sarah hadn't eaten since yesterday. Finally, Sarah nodded reluctantly, and with a final glance towards her son, she headed towards the door with Jazmine following.

They rode the elevator in silence. Emerging from the elevator, Jazz followed Sarah to the cafeteria. Still keeping their thoughts to themselves, they walked along the cafeteria line, looking at the unappetizing food.

Jazz took a muffin from one of the shelves, and then poured herself a large cup of coffee. She watched as Sarah chose a tuna sandwich, and poured a coffee as well. Walking to the cashier, Jazz paid for both of their items.

"Thank you," Sarah said in almost a whisper.

Jazz led the way to a secluded table and sat. She picked at the muffin, while occasionally sipping the coffee. Sarah sat across from her, barely touching the sandwich, but drinking her coffee. Her expression was distant, and her features worn with exhaustion.

"Are you going to be okay to go home?" Jazz said, thinking of what Kirsten had told her about Aidan's father.

Sarah looked up, startled out of her thoughts. "Of course." She answered, looking puzzled by the question.

Jazmine hesitated, knowing that Sarah had misunderstood her question. "I mean will you be safe when you go home?"

"Oh," Sarah said awkwardly, looking down. She hesitated, not comfortable speaking about such things. Finally, she sighed, and nodded. "Yes. I spoke with the police earlier today. He's been arrested, and charged with assault." She said, reluctant to say her husband's name.

Jazz nodded, feeling a little better. "Has this ever happened before?" She asked tentatively.

Sarah looked towards the door before speaking in a low tone. "He's never lost his temper this bad before."

"Does he lose his temper often?"

"He didn't when I first met him; he was so sweet, and kind. After we got married, we started to argue, but everyone argues at first, so I tried not to worry. Things got worse when Aidan was seven. Tyler was laid off from his job, and he started drinking. His temper is worse when he drinks." Sarah said, occasionally breaking her sentences with sips of coffee. "He eventually got a new job, but the money isn't as good, and he hates it, so that doesn't help." It was so easy to make excuses for his behavior. She had always hoped that things would get better, even through all the bad times.

"Did you ever think about leaving him?"

"I thought about it. But he always felt so bad afterwards that I didn't have the heart. He would be so sweet like he used to be." Sarah stared down at her hand, reminiscing about the good days momentarily, before continuing. "Tyler always promised to stop drinking. He kept promising things would change. But they are still promises, and look what has happened now." Sarah stared down into her coffee with a guilty expression.

Jazz reached across the table, and touched her hand. "Hey, none of this is your fault. You have been doing your best." Jazmine said, reassuringly.

Sarah took a few shaky gasps of air, brushing away a tear that escaped. "I don't know what I'll do if he doesn't wake up."

Pushing aside her own doubts, Jazz frowned sternly. "Don't think like that. Aidan will pull through this. He is strong."

Sarah nodded in agreement, and stared down into her coffee cup. They both sipped their coffee in silence, letting their exhausted minds be livened by the caffeine. Jazz tried to think of something to say, but could find no conversation that seemed suitable. Sarah was the first to break the silence between them.

"How long have you and Aidan been dating?"

"It'll be five months in two weeks. We met in September." Jazz said.

"Has it been that long?" Sarah commented, sounding surprised.

Jazz blushed slightly, embarrassed by the length of time that had passed without Sarah's knowledge. "I kept pestering him to introduce me to you, but I guess I understand why he didn't now. But it's nice to meet you finally."

"So are you two serious then?"

"I like to think so." Jazz said shyly.

"My son is lucky to have you," Sarah said, causing Jazz to blush a darker shade of red. Looking more at ease, she took a few bites of her sandwich.

Jazz tore off a small piece of her muffin, chewing it slowly, and then tore off another. She was absorbed by her thoughts, reflecting on her relationship with Aidan. What qualified as serious these days? They had talked about going to the same college, and maybe finding an apartment together. Was that serious or wishful thinking? Maybe she wouldn't even get the chance to find out. She rested her chin in the palm of her hand as she continued to chew mindlessly.

Soon her muffin had vanished, and her coffee had been drained. She toyed with the paper wrapper idly, waiting for Sarah to finish after she glanced at the clock for the tenth time.

"It's been half an hour, should we head back upstairs?" Sarah asked finally.

Jazz nodded, and got up. Clearing the table, she threw the cups in the garbage. She walked with Sarah to the elevator. As the elevator climbed the floors, Jazz began to fidget nervously, trying to imagine what the doctor would say. She glanced at Sarah who looked just as nervous.

Doctor Briggs looked up, and nodded in greeting as they came in. "We are finishing up. If you would like to take a seat, I'll explain the results."

Jazz claimed one of the chairs, and settled herself into it. She chewed on her lower lip nervously as she watched the doctor jot down a few notes on his clipboard. Wrapping her arms around herself, she waited for him to finish.

He said something to the nurse, and the nurse nodded, and departed. The doctor brought the spare chair over again, and sat with them.

"I've finished the tests." Doctor Briggs said, trying to keep his tone positive. "He scored a five out of a possible fifteen. Keeping in mind that this is not an exact science, other patients who scored similarly had a fifty percent chance of remaining in a coma or dying. Patients who do wake up had a thirty-four percent chance of having a good recovery or moderate disability."

Jazz felt her chest tighten, and she forgot to breathe. She looked over towards where Aidan lay motionless. The possibility of losing him seemed to be more and more of a possibility.

"However, given his age, he has a better chance of recovering than someone who is over forty. Another encouraging statistic is that two-thirds of patients can make a good recovery if they are in the coma for less than two weeks. So don't lose hope." Doctor Briggs said.

She looked towards Sarah who appeared as devastated as she did. Jazz took a deep breath, managing to calm herself slowly. They were only numbers. There was always the possibility of beating the odds.

"The good news is that he is continuing to breathe well on his own. Most coma patients have poor oxygen saturation in their blood, but he is doing well. We'll continue to monitor him closely, but we can be positive about that." He said.

Jazz chewed her lip as she listened, trying to feel optimistic about that good news.

"We'll continue to do the tests to track any progress. If you see him open his eyes or make any other movements, notify one of the nurses. It can be a good sign." The doctor said. "Do you have any questions?"

Jazmine glanced at Sarah, giving her the first opportunity to ask a question. When she said nothing, she spoke up. "Could there be long term effects after he wakes up?" She asked, trying to be confident.

"There could be," The doctor admitted. "We won't know for certain until he regains consciousness. Then we can assess if the trauma has caused impairments."

"Do injuries like this usually cause a coma?" Jazmine glanced at Aidan as she spoke. The bruise on his head had darkened to shades of black and blue.

The Doctor hesitated for a moment, finding the right words. "Head traumas are complex. Typically with such as injury, I would have anticipated a concussion," He said, glancing at the chart he had brought in with him. "A coma is a rather unusual response."

Jazmine chewed her lip as the doctor spoke, growing more anxious again.

"Should we be concerned?" Sarah spoke for the first time in a while.

"A loss of consciousness is the body's way of trying to protect the brain. We will continue to monitor him carefully for any changes." The Doctor answered, trying to reassure her.

Jazmine sighed grimly, not feeling any better about things.

"Do you have any more questions for now?" Doctor Briggs asked after they were quiet for a few moments.

Sarah shook her head, and glanced towards Jazz. Shaking her head as well, Jazz looked down at the floor.

The doctor nodded, and stood. "If you have any more questions, I am on shift until midnight. Call a nurse, and they will get in touch with me." Giving them one last encouraging smile, the doctor left them to continue his rounds.

Jazz tried to hide her exhaustion as Sarah looked over at her. Noticing her fatigue, Sarah looked at the time. She was surprised to see that it was nearly nine in the evening.

"It's getting late. You should go home and rest. You can come back, and visit in the morning." Sarah suggested.

Jazz was about to protest when she thought of her parents, and how worried they would be by now. She nodded reluctantly, and got up.

"Try to get some rest too, Mrs. Matheson."

"I will try." She said, glancing over at the cot in the corner of her son's room. As Jazmine gathered her things to leave, she looked over at her. "Please call me Sarah, dear."

Jazmine nodded. "Good night, Sarah." She said as she left.

Nine...

"While there's life, there's hope."
– Marcus Tullius Cicero

After Azriel had left him, Aidan rested for a while before getting up to explore the house. The home was as he would have imagined a house from the nineteenth century. He moved around cautiously, touching the occasional items as he explored the rooms.

It wasn't a mansion, but it was certainly larger than his home. He counted three bedrooms, and the sitting room where he had woken up. He had seen another room upstairs, but passed by the closed door when he heard Azriel moving around inside. He passed a kitchen, but hadn't bothered to investigate much beyond glancing in from the doorway. The vintage kitchen appeared tidy, but looked unused as it lacked any food.

Finding the back door, Aidan stepped out onto the porch. He looked around the backyard, which was shaded by tall trees, and carpeted by wildflowers and lush grass. The garden was surrounded by a stone wall that encircled the house, and an iron gate tucked in the corner.

Twilight lit the garden in a soft orange glow. Taking a deep breath, he expected the smell of flowers, but instead the air smelled like honey. Aidan relaxed slowly, enjoying the wild beauty. It seemed like the type of garden Jazz would like.

His stomach clenched with guilt as he realized it was the first time he had thought of Jazz. How had he forgotten about her? He had checked on his Mom, but he hadn't bothered to look in on her. He cringed, feeling neglectful. She would have known something was wrong when he didn't show up at school.

He started down the brick path towards the wrought iron gate. As he touched the cool metal, he recalled what Azriel had said about leaving the property. He hesitated, considering whether he needed to heed the caution. As he recalled what had happened at the hospital, he acknowledged the necessity reluctantly. Perhaps it would be better to listen.

Aidan turned, and headed back into the house. He returned to the closed door which he had neglected in his earlier exploration of the house. Knocking, he waited in the hallway for a response.

"Come in," Azriel called from within. As Aidan opened the door, and stepped in, Azriel looked up from a book. "Feeling more rested?"

"I am." Aidan answered. "You said if I wanted to leave, I should come find you." His uncertainty about the man was outweighed by his desire to see Jazmine.

Azriel nodded. "Is there somewhere you would like to go?"

"There's someone I would like to visit. Preferably alone." Aidan said tentatively, trying not to feel embarrassed.

"It would be irresponsible to allow you to go alone. I will accompany you, and stay close enough to shield you from being noticed by the Shade, but you will still have your privacy. Is that agreeable?" Azriel said, closing his book and rising.

Aidan arched a brow, surprised by Azriel's compromise. "Really?" He was not accustomed to people being accommodating to his wishes.

"You will find that I am far more agreeable than Asmodeus... or your Father."

Aidan tensed involuntarily at the mention of Tyler, the air suddenly tasting bitter with his anxiety. "What do you know about him?" He said in a low voice.

"I apologize for bringing him up," Azriel said, his voice was soothing, and Aidan couldn't help but relax. "I know about your Father because Asmodeus was sent to guard you. He shared his memories with me."

"Then you know..." Aidan whispered, trying to fight through the strange calm that had taken over him.

"Yes, I do." Azriel acknowledged lowly. "You have my sympathy."

"I don't need you feeling sorry for me." Aidan snapped, his temper flaring. He hated the pity people offered when they viewed him as a victim.

"I did not mean any harm." Azriel looked taken back by his sudden outburst. However, he did not allow the reaction to bother him. "We do not need to speak of it further. We should be going."

Aidan calmed himself, and nodded. "Can you do that teleporting thing that Asmodeus did?"

Azriel nodded. "It is simple enough. Visualize the location where you would like to go."

Aidan closed his eyes, and imagined Jazz's bedroom. It was easy to picture the vibrant colors of her walls. As Aidan focused on his destination, he felt Azriel touch his shoulder, and then the sensation of the now familiar tug.

Once the feeling had passed, he opened his eyes, and looked around the familiar surroundings of Jazmine's dark room. The blue light of her computer tower lit the room with a pale glow. A pile of clothes littered her normally clean floor near the end of her bed. Aidan smiled as he saw Jazz curled up under the blankets, although he was concerned to see that her expression was worried even in her sleep.

"Thanks." He whispered to Azriel, forgetting that his voice would not disrupt Jazmine.

Azriel nodded, and matched his lowered tone when he spoke. "I will wait nearby. Come to find me there when you are ready to leave." Azriel said, and then passed through her door into the hallway.

Aidan approached the bed slowly, and crouched by the edge. He studied her sleeping expression, noticing the worry lines that creased her brow. He reached forward to brush some hair from her face, but his fingers could not feel the strands. He frowned, following the curve of her cheek, though unable to actually touch her.

He continued to trace her features, his fingertips hovering above her skin. Moving carefully, he lay beside her, forgetting that she wouldn't feel his movements.

Aidan breathed in, expecting her sweet scent, but instead, he became aware of her anxiety.

He longed to be able to talk with her again, to be able to touch her again. Holding a simple conversation with her seemed like such a distant hope.

"I miss you so much," Aidan whispered.

Jazz shifted in her sleep, mumbling his name as she slept.

"Jazz?" He said, sitting up a bit. She stirred again, starting to rouse. "Just sleep," Aidan muttered, his mind whirling with possibilities. Could she hear him? He tried to calm the surge of excitement he felt.

He felt a flicker of hope, wondering if it had been a coincidence that she had started to wake the same time he had spoken. He continued to watch her sleep, unwilling to leave her side quite yet. He had plenty of time to talk to Azriel about his suspicions.

~~~~~~~~~

Azriel stood guard out in the hallway, by Jazmine's bedroom door. He listened to the clock on the wall count the seconds as he waited. Time had little influence on him anymore. He remained patient, sensing the connection Aidan had with the girl.

After nearly half an hour had passed, Aidan emerged from the room. Azriel wore a knowing expression, understanding Aidan's disturbed face as he passed through the door. "You will get used to it in time," Azriel said. "Passing through objects will become as natural as walking."

"I don't want to get used to it," Aidan whispered, habitually keeping his voice lowered in the sleeping household. "Remember, I'm trying to get home not become a hunter."

"I understand that. I meant for your time here; you will adjust to it."

Aidan nodded, and Azriel could see him visibly relax. He watched Aidan's expression carefully, noticing how the separation from the girl burdened him. He could sense Aidan's hesitation in asking a question that had clearly made him restless.

"Is something weighing on your mind, Aidan?"

"I think Jazz heard me talking to her. Is that possible?" Aidan answered, trying not to sound too hopeful.

"Whispering that carries to the human realm is possible for an advanced Aduro. However, it is not the type of whisper that a human would wake to." Azriel said cautiously, worrying about the direction of the conversation.

Aidan chewed his lower lip for a time, clearly contemplating his next question carefully.

"You said earlier that most humans cannot see us, but are there some that can?"

Azriel noticed how Aidan's gaze stole towards the bedroom door. Even in the darkness his hopes, and intentions were plain to read. A sigh escaped Azriel, and he took some time to respond to Aidan's question.

"Yes, there are humans who can catch glimpses into our realm. Such a talent is rare, but it does exist." He finally said reluctantly. "But it is dangerous for us to reveal ourselves to them."

Aidan's expression brightened with genuine joy that Azriel had not seen before. The boy's excitement was undeniable, and Azriel could relate to his anticipation of being reunited with a lost love.

Aidan turned, and before Azriel could stop him, he had vanished back into the bedroom. Azriel pursued him. Before Aidan could go to Jazmine's side, Azriel reached out and grabbed hold of his arm roughly.

"Stop," Azriel commanded in a fervent whisper.

"Why?"

"Before you go, and try to rouse her, you should consider the impact that doing so would have on her," Azriel spoke in a low tone, trying to emphasize the seriousness of his statement.

"What are you talking about?" said Aidan, trying not to be drawn in by Azriel's grave tone. Aidan yanked his arm from the firm grip. "I'll explain what is happening, and tell her not to say anything."

"And if someone finds her talking to an empty room?" Azriel countered. "They will think she has gone mad."

"I need to talk to her again. You don't know what it's like..." He insisted.

"Yes, I do." Azriel snapped angrily, cutting him off.

Aidan stepped back, startled by the ferocity of Azriel's sudden temper which was better suited for Asmodeus. He looked towards Jazz as she rolled over, stirring at the sound of the man's voice.

Calming himself, Azriel spoke again in a whisper so he wouldn't disturb her again. "I can't allow you to ruin her life."

"I would never..." Aidan responded quietly, beginning to hesitate now. He looked towards Jazz who had settled into a peaceful sleep again. Azriel related to the tenderness of his expression and sighed.

"I think it is time you heard the story of how Asmodeus and I came to be," Azriel whispered.

"Now?" Aidan frowned, looking towards Jazmine with a torn expression.

"Yes, but not here. You should not wake her until you have heard what I have to say. It may change your mind about revealing yourself." He said gently.

"I'll hear your story, and then decide." He conceded finally.

Azriel nodded. "Good. We'll go to the front room where we won't disturb her."

Turning, Azriel passed through the doorway, and went downstairs without a sound. He slowly eased himself onto the couch that was under the front window. He rubbed his forehead, recalling memories that he had not thought about in many years. His features became heavy with painful emotions as he waited for Aidan to follow him from the room.

Aidan walked a few steps behind Azriel as they made their way to the living room. "So what happened?" He asked, unable to deny his curiosity.

"I will explain," Azriel said, looking uneasy about the prospect. He closed his eyes for a moment, composing himself. Forced to recall the grim details of his human life.

"As a human, my name was David Atkins, and I was born in 1898. In some ways, David's life does not feel like my own, as he existed before Asmodeus and I divided." Azriel said, the memories of his life as David feeling like a painfully familiar story.

"Throughout my human life, I can recall being vaguely aware of this world we are currently in, but I never paid much attention to what I saw or heard. Mostly I only saw flickers of movements, and heard whispered voices. I also became rather adept at judging people's intentions, a well-honed intuition. Gabrielle later explained to me that I was sensing the energy of this world. I was one of the rare humans who could do so."

"Jazz has never mentioned anything like that to me." Aidan interrupted.

Azriel struggled to keep his annoyance at bay. "Would you tell someone if you were hearing, and seeing things that couldn't exist? Things have not changed much in that regard, even since my time. People will still call you mad for such things." He said tensely. "May I continue with the story?"

"Yea. Sorry." Aidan said, leaning back in his chair to listen. Azriel's tone suggested that he let him speak without further interruption.

"In the time that I lived as David, you would be hard-pressed to find any portion of the population that would tolerate talk about such kinds of intuition or spirits, never mind believe in it. Such things were viewed as madness, and became a sure way to visit the asylum. As such, I never spoke of what I sensed or heard for most of my life. In fact, I coped by not acknowledging what my intuition told me. It wasn't until I met Elisabeth Bradford that I began to pay attention to my abilities." Azriel spoke Elisabeth's name with such reverence, and regret that it caused Aidan to lean forward as he became more engrossed with the story.

Azriel looked across the room, his gaze unfocused on his surroundings, as he reminisced over memories of Elisabeth. He recalled her joyful brown eyes, and the blonde ringlets of her hair. Returning to the present, he took a deep breath, and continued with his tale.

"I was introduced to Elisabeth at a party my parents were hosting. She was the purest person I had ever come across in my human life. Goodwill seemed to flow from her. Her laughter was so infectious that it could melt even the coldest of hearts. She was beautiful, but her charm, and good spirit made her even lovelier to me. I became enamored from the moment I met her, and I fell madly in love with her. But I never knew if she shared my affections."

"There was another man who was captured by her charm as well. His name was Damien Kade, and she met him a few weeks after I. Kade and I, had known each other previously, and I had never cared for him much. It wasn't until he learned of my interest in Elisabeth that Kade began to get to know her better. Elisabeth was taken with his charismatic nature as soon as she met him. But he cared only for her outward beauty, paying little attention to her mind or heart." Azriel paused again, Hatred had ingrained Damien's face vividly in his mind. Calming his anger, he continued.

"At first, I thought it was jealousy I was feeling towards Kade, but the more I spoke with him, the more I sensed something evil within him. I heard the whispers of cruel things when I was in his presence, things that made me ill to even think about. I tried to ignore the strange feelings, but they became so overpowering that I was certain Elisabeth would be harmed if I did not try to sever their ties."

"Naturally, I tried to warn her, but Elisabeth thought I was being corrupted by jealousy. She warned me not to make ignorant accusations, saying that I did not know Kade as she did. But I did know him, better than she did in fact. I had been listening to his intentions for months by that point. During those months Elisabeth, and I had grown closer, but she still did not view me in the same light as I viewed her."

"Like a fool, I told her of what I had sensed from Kade. For weeks, I tried to convince her I was speaking the truth, desperate to save her from the fate Damien had planned for her. I became obsessed with trying to protect her. In hindsight, I am sure my ranting had turned me into a madman, but I would never have harmed Elisabeth. And for the first time ever, Elisabeth and I argued. Despite her orders for me to stay away, I continued to visit her. Perhaps that is why it was so easy for everyone to believe Kade's story instead of mine."

"I found Elisabeth murdered a few mornings after our argument. I called the police to report the murder, pointing to Kade as a suspect. However, it was all too convenient for him to place the blame for her murder on me, since I had proven myself to be so crazed days earlier. It was Kade's good name against my blemished name. Ironically, I was saved from the death penalty by Kade's testimony since he recounted what Elisabeth had told him about me. I was found to be mad, and was sentenced to be imprisoned at the Colquitz asylum."

"I spent years in that terrible place. I cannot recall exactly how long it was, but it felt like a lifetime. I knew it was Kade who had murdered Elisabeth, but no one would listen. His good name protected him from the accusations I made. Over the years, my bitterness, and anger began to drive me crazy. Revenge was all I dreamed of for years. I suppose that is when Asmodeus began to take form. I didn't stand a chance of escaping or being released. My only refuge from purgatory was to take my own life. A refuge I ultimately sought..."

Azriel avoided meeting Aidan's horrified expression. He ran his fingers through his hair, tidying any strands that had fallen out of place.

"Asmodeus and I share the same recollection of opening our eyes in the cell, and leaving David's body. At that point, we were still one existence. Passing through the front doors of that place was the greatest sensation of freedom we had ever experienced. With our newfound liberty we left that place and never looked back."

"So what happened to Kade, he got away with it?" Aidan asked, frowning.

"He escaped the law. However, he did not escape punishment entirely. David's lingering need for revenge was so great that we searched for him. We found him eventually. He had settled into a comfortable lifestyle, although we became aware of a number of murders that followed him wherever he went."

"The revenge was slow and sweet. Life became so unbearable for Kade that he eventually also took his own life. These days were the early days of Asmodeus. I can recall only fragments of my own existence at that time. I had no stomach for what Asmodeus did, and perhaps that is why David split as he had."

"His, or rather our, mind had become fragile during the time in the asylum. He craved revenge so badly that his fury was an undeniable force. David had always been a good man in life, and his morals carried past death. Two personas began to emerge from his conflicted views. He could not enact his revenge while his moral compass still guided him, so he abandoned morality in favor of action for one persona. In the other persona, he invested all his goodness. In this way, David was able to balance his need to become both evil and divine, but in doing so, he also abandoned himself."

"With David's lingering thirst for revenge satiated, Asmodeus's control faded, and my own being came to the forefront. It was shortly after that when Gabrielle found me wandering, and took pity. If she had met Asmodeus first, I am certain she would have destroyed us. However, she took mercy on me. She agreed to train me as long as Asmodeus could be kept under control. Gabrielle has tolerated him since because she recognizes him as a valuable weapon against the Shades. He is still as bitter, and angry as the day of Elisabeth's death. I thought revenge would satisfy him. However that does not seem to be the case." Azriel let out a heavy sigh, the recounting of the tale having taken its toll on him emotionally.

"Do you understand now why it is important that you think about your decision? You should not wish any fate on Jazmine that you would not be willing to endure yourself." Azriel said gravely. "She could stand to lose a lot if you revealed our world to her."

"Times have changed." Aidan objected. "There are plenty of people who believe in the supernatural now."

"Yes, times have changed, but have they changed enough to save her from ridicule? This is your time. You would know better than I." Azriel rose from his seat slowly. "I will not stop you from visiting her again if you deem it suitable. I have made you aware of the possible consequences. I will wait here until you are ready to return home."

He watched as Aidan rose, and headed up the stairs again. Aidan stopped halfway, plagued by uncertainty. Azriel could sense his hesitation, but did nothing to sway his decision. Finally, Aidan turned back towards him, his expression defeated.

"Let's go." He said.

Azriel nodded, trying not to let his relief show. "It is time we began your training anyway." He said gently.

Ten...

"Knowledge is of no value unless you put it into practice."
– Anton Chekhov

"Again." Azriel insisted.

"I can't." Aidan hissed, his frustration fueling his temper to rise.

Since leaving Jazmine's home three days earlier, they had been training consistently within the garden walls of Azriel's home. They had only taken brief breaks to replenish the energy lost during training by sipping the shimmering liquid from a crystal decanter.

Despite having not slept for days, Aidan found that he had no desire for sleep. He was continuously surprised by how effective the drink was at chasing away the weariness he felt. All his other human needs vanished as well, including hunger, and thirst, even the need to breathe had been reduced to a habit rather than a requirement. Everything in this world depended only on the amount of energy contained within his soul. This self-sufficient existence allowed for the frustrating task of training to continue as long as Azriel deemed necessary. His current lack of progress only added to Aidan's frustration. The only variation in their routine was a change in the skills they focused on developing.

It was that frustration which caused him to turn away from Azriel, and retreat to where the decanter was on the stone bench. Sitting heavily, he poured himself a glass of the drink, and breathed in the lavender scent which calmed him. He took a sip and felt his energy restore slowly.

Azriel allowed the break, and sat beside Aidan. He poured a small dose of liquid for himself, and took a slow sip. They sat in silence as they watched the sun descend towards the horizon.

Azriel glanced at his pupil. "We need a diversion," Azriel said after a few minutes of easy silence. With a wave of his hand, Azriel crafted a chess set between them. "Do you play?" He asked, indicating the board.

"I know the rules," Aidan said, glancing at the translucent pieces. He could practically hear his Mom's voice as he recalled how she had explained the rules, and movements of the game.

"Knowing the rules is essential to any game," Azriel said with a cryptic smile. Extending his hand slightly, he indicated that Aidan should go first.

Aidan had only studied the board for a moment before making his first move hastily. Azriel answered the move with more patience. The moves continued to transpire in a similar pattern.

"Do you enjoy chess?" Azriel asked.

"It is a difficult game for having such simple rules," Aidan observed and Azriel nodded in agreement.

"It is." He agreed. "Each opponent changes how the game is played." With steady patience, Azriel moved towards checkmate, planning numerous moves ahead. "It's a game based on knowing your opponent, and being steps ahead of them." Azriel reasoned, watching Aidan's expression carefully as he prepared his trap.

Aidan looked over the board quickly before spotting his move. He grinned victoriously as he captured Azriel's queen. Azriel accepted the loss of the queen graciously, knowing that the sacrifice would help secure his impending victory. "Aggression can be an effective strategy for some, but sometimes sacrifices must be made for the greater goal." He reasoned. He countered Aidan's move with ease, and announced checkmate with his next move.

Aidan seemed surprised by the sudden defeat, and then shrugged it off. "Guess strategy isn't my thing." He admitted.

Azriel chuckled knowingly. "It is an acquired skill." Allowing the chess pieces to vanish, he looked at Aidan expectantly. "Shall we resume training?"

"Do we have to?" Aidan asked, sounding reluctant.

"You are making progress," Azriel said encouragingly.

Aidan sighed. "It doesn't feel like I am."

During the past few days, Azriel had repeatedly put Aidan to the test of resisting his influence. Training had been an roller coaster of highs and lows. Azriel's sway urged him to feel a vast spectrum of emotions.

"You have mastered recognizing, and blocking an obvious influence. It is only countering the more subtle attempts which eludes you now."

"What's the point? How is this going to help me learn how to defend myself?"

"You need to be aware of when you are being influenced. A Shade can influence your emotions, as well as attack you physically. The first step to defending yourself is to perceive the attack." Azriel paused for a moment to take another sip of his drink.

"Be assured that you are making progress, and rapidly at that. I have heard of apprentices taking longer to simply be aware of when they are being influenced, and even longer to block it. Gabrielle must be aware of your natural ability, which is why she has chosen you for whatever task she has in mind."

"And what exactly does she have in mind? Why can't she send me back?" Aidan grumbled.

"Gabrielle's mind is her own. When she feels you are ready, she will share the knowledge. You can trust her judgment; she has far more experience than you can imagine."

"Why do you think she chose me? It's not like I'll be stronger than you or Asmodeus anytime soon."

"Your modesty is honourable; however, don't place so little value on your skills. You are a strong individual, even if foolishly stubborn." He responded kindly causing Aidan to fidget uncomfortably, unaccustomed to being spoken to with kind words.

"If you say so," Aidan said gruffly, rubbing the back of his neck.

"I do. Beyond a strong character, you also have unique circumstances. Your human body is still alive, and yet you are in our realm. This has never occurred before to my knowledge, so that gives me faith in Gabrielle's interest in you."

Aidan still looked unconvinced, but nodded reluctantly. He avoided speaking again by draining his glass, and then setting it back on the stone table. Looking towards the horizon again, he watched the sun sink lower.

Azriel mimicked Aidan and finished his drink. Rather than staying seated, he rose and glanced towards the sun. "We should continue." He commented, unfazed by the scowl Aidan gave him.

"Fine," Aidan said, and started to rise.

"You can stay where you are. Close your eyes and relax."

Aidan nodded, and settled back onto the bench. He did as instructed, and closed his eyes, trying to hold onto his own emotions while relaxing. He affixed his scowl adamantly to his features, intent on staying frustrated. He focused on his thoughts and emotions, ever vigilant of when Azriel's influence would creep into his mind.

As he waited, he began to feel more and more frustrated. Aidan shifted restlessly where he sat. He couldn't stand any of this. All he wanted to do was go home, and return to some semblance of normality. This wasn't his world, and he didn't belong here. Why couldn't they send him back as he wanted? Gabrielle had no right to hold him ransom with a task before she would send him home. She could probably send do it now if she tried hard enough. Aidan crossed his arms over his chest.

He fumed for a few minutes longer before he realized what was happening. Azriel had manipulated his already existing frustration into anger. Now that he was aware of it, he could recall the way the foreign aggression had crept into his mind.

Taking a slow deep breath, Aidan pushed the negative emotions away. The frustration tried to linger, but Aidan numbed himself to the feelings. He was well practiced at retreating from his emotions, and found the technique useful now. He felt a final push against his defense as Azriel made another attempt, but Aidan kept his emotional wall strong.

"Well done!" Azriel praised, his expression bright with approval.

Aidan smiled a bit, trying to rein in the pride that was threatening to overtake him. "Thanks." He muttered, running his fingers through his hair self-consciously.

"Let us keep practicing," Azriel said, still looking proud.

By the time dawn was nearing, Aidan had mastered the ability to detect Azriel's influence and block it. He could not deny the glimmer of pride he felt at his accomplishment, but still shied away from Azriel's compliments.

"You are improving quickly," his mentor commented as they returned to the stone bench again. "You should be able to defend yourself from the influence of most Shade or Aduro you come across now."

"I thought the Aduro were good. Why do I need to shield myself from them?" Aidan questioned.

"The Aduro are good. However, you should never abandon your ability to think on your own. The Aduro are not infallible, and can make mistakes as well. Remember that." Azriel suggested his expression thoughtful for a moment. "But given your progress, I think it is time for you to meet Gabrielle."

≈≈≈≈≈≈≈≈≈

"Why did you drop us so far away?" Aidan asked, glancing at Azriel who walked beside him. They hadn't been walking for long through the downtown streets, but it seemed pointless given that Azriel could have brought them directly to their destination.

They approached the cathedral at a slow pace. Even from a few blocks away, the cathedral's presence pulled all attention away from the surrounding buildings. Aidan had noticed the giant stone building downtown before, but honestly had never paid much attention to it, until now.

"Because I wanted the opportunity to offer you some advice concerning Gabrielle," Azriel responded, taking an earnest tone which Aidan had not heard from him before.

Suddenly wary. Aidan's stomach twisted into a tighter knot with every step taken towards the cathedral. The mention of Gabrielle had him feeling shaky with nerves. If he had found himself in this situation days earlier, his skin would have felt cold and clammy.

"Gabrielle is kind, but address her respectfully and politely. Do not reject her influence, but do not be manipulated by it either."

"Is that why you taught me how to block influences before I met her?" Aidan said, looking at Azriel curiously. Azriel gave no direct answer; rather he motioned for Aidan to proceed. He did not speak as they were ascending the exterior steps of the cathedral, and stood outside the large wooden doors.

"A final caution, do not be captivated by her charms." Leading him to the staircase at the base of the bell tower of the church. Zacharias was absent from his post, but Azriel was unconcerned. The guard was always nearby.

"Is she expecting me?"

"No, but she will welcome you," Azriel replied. Reaching the stairs, Azriel stopped and motioned for him to continue.

"Aren't you coming with me?" Aidan stammered, intimidated at the thought of meeting Gabrielle alone.

Azriel shook his head. "This is a journey you need to make on your own. I will wait here. You have nothing to fear, Aidan. Go to the top of the staircase, and she will be waiting."

With Azriel's advice in mind, Aidan started up the spiraling staircase. His steps were slow and timid. He was glad that there was no echo of his footsteps off the walls. Nearing the top, he took a deep breath to steady his nerves, and then took the final steps with forced confidence.

The empty bell tower was filled with the sunrise's golden light. White gossamer curtains were draped around the windows and flowed down to the floor. A breeze from the window caused them to blow gently. If he concentrated hard enough, Aidan was almost certain he could catch a glimpse of a pastel shade of blue which betrayed the wisps of the breeze flowing through the curtains.

Above him, the iron cast bells hung in the center of the room, its rope dangling down. Elegant furniture and lush plants decorated the room. Golden threads embroidered the silk cushions of a nearby settee which was nestled under a window. Outside the window, songbirds greeted the morning with cheerful melodies. It seemed that Gabrielle had a little piece of heaven to herself. However, there was a cold emptiness to the room despite the fine furnishings.

"Gabrielle?" Aidan called out, chiding himself mentally for the waver in his voice. Advancing farther into the room, Aidan looked around, but found that he was alone. Braver now, he ventured over to one of the windows to take in the view of the city.

The early sunlight washed the city in a warm orange light. It was a beautiful sight, and he felt himself be soothed by the atmosphere. He leant against the window frame and took in the serene sight. With the sun on his face, the room became noticeably warmer, and he couldn't help, but be calmed.

"Greetings, Aidan. Welcome to my home." A female voice said behind him. Aidan straightened quickly, and turned to face Gabrielle.

"I..." He started to say, but was interrupted by Gabrielle's appearance. She possessed such ageless beauty that he could not help but be distracted despite Azriel's warning. Her dark hair tumbled down past her shoulders in loose curls, framing her delicate features. She wore a black silk dress, which offset her pale complexion. Despite the conservative design, the dress accented the curves of her figure. Recovering from his surprise, Aidan finally spoke.

"Thank you. It is a pleasure to meet you." Aidan said, trying to recall every ounce of politeness his mother had taught him.

Gabrielle smiled, and Aidan grinned foolishly back. He felt like a young boy talking to his first crush. The room felt warmer, and he found it easy to relax in her presence, despite his giddiness. Azriel had made her sound intimidating, but he could not imagine her gentle voice ever rising in anger.

"I have been looking forward to meeting you," Gabrielle said gently, her bare feet silent on the floor as she approached him. She embraced him in a motherly hug.

"It is unfortunate that we have to meet under such circumstances. I would have rather met you under joyous ones." She said as she released him slowly. Holding onto his shoulders, she stepped back, and looked him over at arm's length. "You look well."

"Thank you," Aidan said politely, trying to gather his thoughts enough to think clearly in her presence. "I have been waiting to meet you as well. Azriel said you would be able to help me get home."

"It is within my power, but it is not so simple, unfortunately." Gabrielle's expression turned troubled, and she walked to the window, looking out over the city. "It is not your burden to bear, but…"

Aidan interrupted her quickly, hating to see her troubled. "But, I would like to help." He said without hesitation, surprised by his own eagerness, though not concerned by it. The reward of seeing Gabrielle's expression brighten was the only reassurance he needed to know that he had made the right choice.

"You are as generous as I suspected you would be," Gabrielle said warmly.

"But, why me?"

"To put it simply, you are unique. I foresaw your arrival years ago, and had been waiting for you. Although I wish your it had not been as a result of such unfortunate events." She commented. "Even if you do not know it, Aidan, you are powerful. So powerful in fact that it is your destiny is to serve a great purpose in this realm."

Aidan arched an eyebrow skeptically, but said nothing. He was sure it would be rude to disagree with her despite his disbelief.

Gabrielle's whimsical laugh filled the room as she interpreted his expression. "True heroes never believe they are destined for greatness until they are forced to seize it. Do not feel bad about doubting me; I only ask that you have faith in my judgment of you."

Aidan remained unconvinced, but could not bring himself to deny her. "I have faith in you." He mumbled, fighting against the shyness that threatened to overwhelm him. "But, what destiny could I possibly have?"

"Let us sit comfortably, and I will explain." Gabrielle moved to the settee, and settled on the plump cushions. Only when Aidan joined her did she speak again. "I presume you were tutored in the history of our realm, and the present war with the Shade."

"Yes, but I'm no soldier and my training would take too long. Besides, how much of a difference can I make in a war?" Aidan spoke quickly.

Gabrielle listened to his objections for a moment before holding up her hand to silence him. "You are so quick to deny your abilities." She said, her tone hinting at disapproval. "Tell me about your training first, and then I will reveal your intended destiny."

"Azriel explained the rules of this world to me. He also explained about the Aduro and Shade."

"Good, and you understand his lessons?"

Aidan nodded, and Gabrielle's expectant look suggested there was another topic she desired to discuss.

"And what of your combat training with Asmodeus?"

"I haven't started training with Asmodeus yet," Aidan said, pretending to be distracted by the birds outside the window to disguise his apprehension. He had no desire to train with Asmodeus. Judging by his less than tolerant nature, he would make a harsh instructor. He much preferred Azriel's calmer tutelage. He already felt some measure of trust, and respect for the man.

"Azriel has been teaching me how to detect and block influences."

"So you have received no combat training?" Gabrielle inquired intently.

Aidan shook his head, and looked back towards her. For a brief moment, he thought he saw a flash of anger in her eyes. The expression was gone before he could be sure.

"Azriel thought it was best that I be able to defend myself before I began to learn combat techniques," Aidan said quickly in defense of Azriel's decision.

"A rather logical progression of training," Gabrielle commented, although there was a tautness at the corner of her mouth. "I will speak with Azriel about his intended curriculum. I trust that you are in capable hands with your instructors."

"He is an excellent teacher." He responded, uncertain if Gabrielle was displeased with Azriel. Aidan hesitated then focused on her energy.

He could feel the calm overtone of her mood like a pleasant breeze radiating from beside him. But, under the pleasantness, he sensed a flame of anger burning steadily. Taking a deep breath, he focused on it, wishing to calm her, he suspected the anger was directed at Azriel. He thought he was making no progress when he felt a shock of delight overtake her rage.

"Oh, my darling, Aidan. You doubt yourself, and yet you already attempt to influence me." She crooned proudly, as she grinned at him.

"I am sorry, I shouldn't have," Aidan said quickly, his cheeks flushing with embarrassment.

"Do not apologize, my dear. Your intentions were honourable enough. Besides, this proves my point that you are the one for whom I have been waiting. It is only days into your training, and you are attempting to influence me, which is not an easy feat."

Uncomfortable with Gabrielle's flattery, Aidan fidgeted and looked away. "So why have you been waiting for me?"

Gabrielle's mood sobered at his question. "It is a terrible burden which I place on you. If this were a task I could complete myself, I would. Sadly, I cannot do this alone." Gabrielle sighed remorsefully before continuing. "There is an individual who is so powerful that if he becomes an ally of the Shade, I fear that the war will be lost. Beyond that, I am humbled to say that his power has exceeded my own, and hinders my ability to return you home. He is determined to keep you here permanently. I hope to help you avoid this fate, but I cannot do it alone."

"But if he is too powerful for you, then how am I going to defeat him?"

"Trust my judgment of your strength, but also know that we will face him together," Gabrielle assured him, placing her hand over his. "Will you pledge to help me?"

"I have to if I want to go home. So yes." Aidan said, thinking of his mother and Jazz.

"I am in your debt," Gabrielle said graciously. "Continue with your training, and when you are prepared, I will call on you to test your abilities." She said, rising from where she was seated.

Standing as well, Aidan was suddenly nervous. "Gabrielle, who is this enemy?"

"I do not wish to distract you from your training with unnecessary thoughts of him. Focus on your training, and trust me. Can you do so?"

When he nodded, Gabrielle looked pleased. "Excellent." As they parted, Gabrielle kissed his forehead. "Until we meet again, Aidan." She said pleasantly as she released him.

Eleven...

"What you cannot enforce, do not command."
– Sophocles

Azriel surveyed the interior of the church from his location beside one of the stone pillars. He was bathed in a spectrum of pale colors from the stain glass windows behind him. The serenity of the church calmed him, and his quiet presence added to the atmosphere of the building.

As the door to the church was opened, Azriel's gaze was attracted there. He watched as an old man started down the aisle, leaning on his cane. The white-haired man was breathing heavily as he finally reached the middle section of pews, and sank to his knees there.

Captivated now, Azriel left his position by the pillar, and approached the old man. He strode silently down the aisle, and stood at the entrance of the pew where the man sat. Soon he lost all track of time as he observed the man, his attention focused on the weight of sorrow suffocating him. The very air seemed oppressive, so Azriel laid a comforting hand on the elderly man's shoulder. Although the man did not react to his touch, his shoulders slackened as some of his burdens appeared to ease. Azriel removed his hand, keeping a silent vigil beside the man.

"Azriel?"

Hearing his name, Azriel looked over his shoulder, and saw Aidan standing awkwardly in the aisle a few feet away.

"Finished already?"

"I was gone for a while," Aidan whispered, glancing awkwardly at the elderly man.

"I apologize. I lost track of time." Azriel said, taking notice of Aidan's awkwardness. "He cannot hear us." He assured him.

"Why is he here?" Aidan said.

"He has come for comfort and prayer. His wife is very ill, and I imagine they have been together for a very long time." Azriel said respectfully.

"Can we do something for him?"

"Only provide the comfort of our presence. People come to churches for comfort and that is our task here." Azriel glanced at Aidan. "Will you stay with him? I must speak with Gabrielle before we depart." When Aidan nodded, Azriel patted his shoulder, and then started for the bell tower stairs.

≈≈≈≈≈≈≈≈≈

Reaching the top of the stairs, Azriel stepped into a patch of sunlight. He closed his eyes momentarily as the bright rays warmed him. Across the room, he saw Gabrielle basking in a similar sunspot on the settee.

"Good afternoon, Gabrielle." He said, bowing his head respectfully.

Rising from the settee, and crossing the room, Gabrielle smiled in welcome. "I wasn't expecting you, Azriel."

"I find that difficult to believe," Azriel said with a touch of humor in his voice. He had found that there was little Gabrielle did not anticipate.

Gabrielle kissed his cheek. "I trust you are well. What grants me the pleasure of your company?"

"I wished to speak to you about Aidan." He responded after a moment of hesitation.

Gabrielle's smile faded slightly, but her pleasant nature did not disappear entirely. "I imagine you wish to express the same concerns which Asmodeus has already conveyed rather bluntly?"

"I believe so."

With a sigh, Gabrielle nodded, and returned to the settee. "Sit and we shall discuss the matter, although I anticipate the same conclusion."

"Thank you," Azriel said, taking a seat beside her.

"Do not thank me. I only tolerate your inquiry because you have always served me well, and treated me with proper respect, unlike your defiant counterpart."

"Forgive Asmodeus's insolence. I fear that respect for authority has never been in his nature." Azriel looked mildly embarrassed as he spoke about his alter ego.

"Clearly," Gabrielle said cryptically, recalling how Asmodeus frequently tested the limits of her patience. "But let us return to discussing your concerns."

With Gabrielle's encouragement, Azriel turned their conversation back to Aidan. "Aidan has shown great promise in his training, but I wonder if even limitless training will prepare him for this task."

"You are fond of him," Gabrielle observed.

"I am," Azriel admitted. "His life has been full of difficulties, and he does not deserve further struggles." His brow furrowed as he thought back to what he had observed of Aidan's life. No one should treat his or her child like that.

"I know, he is fond of you as well." She responded. "Which will only make his task more difficult I am afraid."

"How will his task become difficult? I thought Asmodeus and I would be aiding him? He is inexperienced. We cannot abandon him in his time of need."

"Unfortunately, as he begins his journey back into the human realm, none of us can assist him. This is why Aidan must be trained properly to be able to protect himself."

"And what is this task you wish to send him on?"

"Truly it is a test, to ensure that he will be ready, but he will be aiding me greatly at the same time," Gabrielle said.

"Will this task be dangerous?"

"It is, which is why Asmodeus must train Aidan in combat."

"Surely I can complete this task for you, and spare Aidan the trouble." Azriel offered.

Gabrielle's musical laughter rang out like soft bells. "Oh Azriel, if you were capable of completing this task, I would have asked you long ago. However, only Aidan can complete this for me."

"Can you enlighten me about this mystery, Gabrielle? I fear to send Aidan into the unknown inadequately prepared."

Gabrielle touched Azriel's cheek, concern flickering across her expression. "Trust me Azriel. It is better if you do not know. I am sure Aidan will be well prepared, though."

Carefully Azriel studied her expression, puzzling over her somber mood. He dismissed it quickly as concern regarding Aidan's situation. "As you command, Gabrielle."

"This is a good opportunity to remind Asmodeus that he should be training Aidan in combat. Your lessons have been beneficial, but combat instruction is long past due." Gabrielle commented, her tone sharp as her thoughts turned to Asmodeus. "Remind him of my command, and that I will not be pleased if he disobeys again."

"Yes, Gabrielle," Azriel said, rising from the settee and bowing to her.

Twelve...

"People who fly into a rage always make a bad landing."
- Will Rogers

"Have you learned nothing?" Asmodeus demanded scornfully, turning his back on Aidan in disgust.

"When the student hasn't learned, the teacher hasn't taught," Aidan responded tersely, recalling his grandmother's phrase. He had never cared much for her many sayings, but he found this one particularly useful as he watched Asmodeus look back to scowl at him.

"Perhaps the student is too dense." He suggested, causing Aidan to glare in return.

"Repeat the lesson to me," Asmodeus demanded.

Aidan cited his earlier lesson almost verbatim to Asmodeus's original explanation. After each failed session, Asmodeus had made him repeat the words. "Objects can be crafted by using the energy created by emotions. For combat, weapons and shields can be crafted. The maker shapes the object's form, but the power of the emotion will affect how strong the object is."

"So you have been paying attention. You only seem to lack the fortitude to complete the task. Now demonstrate a shield, if you can." Asmodeus said skeptically, sitting on a bench nestled in the safety of his garden. Crossing his arms over his chest, he fixed his critical gaze on Aidan.

Closing his eyes, Aidan began to imagine his shield. The shape was simple enough, modelled after the Trojan warrior's equipment. The memory was clear in his mind as he had recently watched a movie about the Trojan war.

Holding the vivid image in his mind, Aidan began to trace its shape in the air with his hands. As his creation began to take shape, he infused it with his emotions. This time, he focused on his memory of Jazz, and his yearning to see her again. All of this would be worth it if he could make it home to her.

Opening his eyes, Aidan adjusted the shield to rest on his arm. He tested the sturdiness of the shield with a knock, and was pleased with his progress. This shield felt heavier, and more real than any of his previous creations. Thinking of Jazz seemed to build strong weapons. Feeling confident, Aidan faced Asmodeus, and nodded.

Rising from the bench, Asmodeus put out his hand, grasping at the air. The hilt of a sword appeared in his hand. A shimmering blue blade materialized between his fingertips as he drew his hand the length of the weapon.

Aidan took the defensive stance that he had been taught, and lifted the shield. He had barely protected himself when Asmodeus struck. The blow landed in the center of the shield, and it shattered almost immediately under the impact. Aidan fell back, rolling out of the way of the blade.

Asmodeus looked furious as the broken pieces of the shield faded from sight. "Do you not possess a single passionate feeling? Look at your weak creations; they wouldn't stand up to the lightest of tests." He scoffed indignantly.

"How do you expect me to win against you when I'm only allowed a shield? You have a sword, and could kill me in one move." Aidan snapped, hating the implication that his feelings for Jazz were weak.

"You could defeat me with a shield based solely on how strong your creation is. However, that doesn't seem likely given your lack of effort. You will be allowed to practice with a sword when you have proven to me you are capable of crafting a strong one." Asmodeus responded coldly.

"What good will weapons do me even if they are strong? I have no idea how to handle a sword. It would take years for me to learn to defend myself against someone." Aidan growled, seething at Asmodeus's indignation.

"You still limit yourself to the rules of the human realm. Forget that world or you will die here." Asmodeus lifted the sword in his hand, and inspected its edge. "In this realm, only the power of your will matters. This sword is a manifestation of my emotions and will. It is not the edge of this blade that will harm you, but my intention behind it. With each strike, our wills are tested, and the weaker weapon gives way, thereby draining your strength. In real combat, one of the fighters would eventually be unable to manifest a weapon, and he would be at the mercy of his opponent."

"What if I were stabbed?"

"Injuries with weapons drain energy faster, but are not usually fatal on their own. You will heal quickly if you can replenish the lost energy. Otherwise, the wound will slowly leech away your strength. But a lesson in healing is better suited to Azriel's guidance." Asmodeus advised, reluctant to admit that his own healing skills were lacking.

Aidan took a deep breath, still trying to come to terms with the new concept of combat. It was strange to exist in a world where the weapon did not matter as much as the emotions you felt. Yet it inspired some hope that he could learn to fight reasonably well if technique did not matter so much.

Thinking of Jazmine, he crafted his shield once again. He prepared himself to meet Asmodeus's blow. He felt the sword strike against the shield, and his arm ached under the blow, but the shield did not give way. As their weapons met, he became aware of the clash of their wills. He felt Asmodeus's iron will and cold emotion as their creations maintained contact. He felt his confidence falter, and the shield vanished immediately.

Asmodeus snarled in a fury, and struck at a nearby bush, causing the shrub to wilt under his strike. "Stupid boy! Not only are your emotions weak, but your character is as well."

Aidan glowered furiously in response. Asmodeus dared to suggest that his love for Jazmine was not strong? How could he know of his feelings for her? She was the one steady thing in his life, always patient, and kind, but fierce in her own right. If anything he failed to do her memory justice. How could he recall her properly when he was trapped in this world where he couldn't see or touch her?

Anger consumed him, and he glared at Asmodeus. Instead of being with Jazmine he had to listen to Asmodeus's insults. Drawing on his fury, he crafted a sword and struck at his instructor. Asmodeus blocked the blow easily. He started to laugh as Aidan struck at him again and again.

"Some improvement at last," Asmodeus said while continuing to block Aidan's hasty blows. "Although you still lack any technique." He commented, lessening his prior praise.

"Nothing I do is ever good enough for you." Aidan panted between haphazard blows, exhausting himself as he tried unsuccessfully to land a strike. He found that he still maintained the habit of wanting to breathe, his mind still clinging to the essentials of his human life.

"Because you still have much to learn," Asmodeus answered, completely unaffected by their fast-paced sparring.

"Well, you aren't a very good teacher." Aidan raged, gathering his remaining strength for a final assault. With all his might he brought the sword against Asmodeus's weapon. He pressed against his teacher's blade, his sword meeting flesh as Asmodeus was surprised by the ferocity of his attack. The edge of his blade cut deeply into his skin, and darkness glared out from the wound. Aidan grinned with satisfaction, unable to deny his pleasure at finally inflicting an injury upon his opponent.

Shock registered on Asmodeus's expression before he pushed Aidan away with a hiss. Still basking in his satisfaction, Aidan allowed his sword to dissolve. Aidan's triumph was short lived as Asmodeus snarled with unbridled fury. Asmodeus lunged towards Aidan. With one sweeping motion, he took out Aidan's legs, and brought him to the ground. His free hand closed around Aidan's throat, pinning him. His knuckles turned white as Asmodeus's other hand tightened on the hilt of his blade.

Aidan struggled under his grip, confusion, and fear stealing away all rational thought. As he looked up at Asmodeus's crazed expression he wondered if he was going to kill him. Fearing for his life, he began to struggle harder; fear burning within him.

He pulled at Asmodeus's wrist with both hands, but could not loosen the grip. He glared up at Asmodeus, suddenly thankful that the lack of air did not weaken him in this realm. Slowly Asmodeus brought the blade forward until the fuller of the blade rested against the skin on Aidan's arm.

Aidan felt his fear turn to anger, and he pulled harder at Asmodeus's hand. An insatiable fury awoke in him, and he was distantly aware of being surprised by the sudden power of the emotion. It was like a fire burned in his belly, consuming him with rage for which he needed an outlet.

He was so distracted by his hatred that he could not pay attention to the unexplained origin of the anger. He was only aware of his sudden hatred for Asmodeus. He despised everything about him, from the way he spoke to how he acted. If he had not been pinned to the ground, he would have tried to strike a killing blow, and that realization should have startled him, but it didn't.

Was it Asmodeus he hated? Once again, he was too weak to defend himself. He had always found himself in the same situation with his father, too weak to defend himself or his mother. Perhaps it was his own shortcomings which caused him to be so weak.

Slowly his hatred for Asmodeus faded away, and his resentment turned inward. He had spent his whole life trying in vain to protect himself. Why should he bother any longer? He found himself wishing that it would all end. Gradually his struggles stopped until he lay still, surrendering to his self-loathing.

As his struggles ceased, Asmodeus released him, and stood. As soon as they were no longer in contact, Aidan's self-hatred vanished, along with the anger he had felt before. He blinked, stunned that such powerful feelings could vanish in an instant. Asmodeus looked down at him scornfully.

"What was that?" Aidan asked, still reeling from the strange waves of emotions that had overtaken him. Now that he was free of such feelings, he could see that they had not been his own, despite the fact that they had felt genuine at the time. He had truly hated himself for a few moments.

"You still have much to learn, kid," Asmodeus said scornfully, allowing his sword to vanish. "Never use anger to attack someone, especially a Shade, unless you are certain your anger is more powerful. Otherwise, they will turn your anger against you."

"That's what that was?" Aidan asked, feeling emotionally exhausted. He shook his head slowly, still confused as to how emotions which weren't his own, had felt so real. Slowly he sat up, wrapping his arms around his knees.

"What you felt initially was my own power fueled by anger," Asmodeus said dully as if the emotional storm was a common experience. Aidan stared at him, stunned that Asmodeus could appear so calm if he possessed such rage. "Then you felt the effects of what I can do when I direct that power against you. Fury is a powerful force when turned into passion."

"I am a Shade, and therefore feed off such emotions. By attacking with anger you only add to my strength. If you had attacked an Aduro with that anger, you might have won. However, I doubt you will be fighting an Aduro, so don't bother using your anger." He advised. "Stick to attacking with positive emotions during our combat. That is how you will weaken a Shade."

As he finished speaking, his gaze became distant as if he was listening to a quiet voice. Aidan watched him curiously as Asmodeus rolled his eyes. Then his entire demeanor began to change. His posture relaxed, and his expression softened into a calm appearance. The darkness which oozed from Asmodeus's wounded arm shifted into pure light.

"Asmodeus?" Aidan asked, uncertain about what he had witnessed.

"Asmodeus is gone for the moment," Azriel responded in a pleasant tone that made Aidan relax. Noticing his own wounded arm, Azriel closed his eyes for a moment, and the wound stitched together.

"I thought Asmodeus was supposed to train me."

"He is, but I thought I should provide a lesson given what occurred. It is important for you to understand the consequences of our world, not just combat. Unfortunately, Asmodeus does not have the patience for such lessons, which is why he suggested I tutor you in this matter."

Aidan nodded, and climbed slowly to his feet. He wavered slightly, feeling unsteady on his feet. Azriel placed a hand on his shoulder, steadying him.

"But first, you must replenish your energy," Azriel said as he retrieved a goblet, and decanter. "Drink, and then we will go."

Thirteen...

*"If you are patient in one moment of anger,
you will escape a hundred days of sorrow."*
– *Chinese Proverb*

The courtyard of the jail was full of subdued activity. Inmates engaged in various activities as they enjoyed their hour in the sunshine. Some played basketball, while others lifted weights, or chatted in small groups. Cameras swept the courtyard at steady intervals, monitoring the yard's activities. Despite the apparent calm of the yard, each inmate was prepared for trouble at a moment's notice. Such was their daily life in prison, where overcrowding caused tempers to run hot, and boil over at the slightest provocation.

It was in the middle of this courtyard that Azriel and Aidan appeared. At first Aidan was puzzled by their location, but then realization dawned on him. Azriel watched as Aidan gained his bearings, and searched the courtyard for a familiar face. The boy's expression hardened as he picked his father out of the sea of orange outfits.

Tyler wasn't difficult to spot as he had separated himself from the other inmates, choosing to sit on the bench of a metal picnic table alone. He crossed his arms over his chest, and wore his usual hard expression. It seemed that nothing had changed, despite the situation in which Aidan had found himself. Did his father even care about what he had done?

"Why are we here?" Aidan said sharply, glancing at Azriel accusingly.

"I brought you here so you can experience how our actions influence the world around us. If you choose to fight with anger, you need to understand the consequences." Azriel said grimly, observing the surroundings.

"What am I supposed to do?" Aidan responded reluctantly. He shifted uncomfortably, watching the inmates warily.

"Whatever you wish, I am not to interfere with what you choose to do."

"Good," Aidan answered, his voice tight with barely withheld anger. Clenching his fist, he strode across the courtyard towards his father. His mind whirled with years of pent-up rage. Here was his opportunity for revenge in a situation where Tyler couldn't harm him in return.

Reaching Tyler, he struck out with a clenched fist. His hand passed through his father's cheek, however, unable to make physical contact with him. He let out a shout of frustration and anger.

"Do you even care what you've done?" He yelled, continuing to lash out at his father despite being unable to touch him. "I'm a vegetable, and you're sitting there looking as smug as ever." Aidan continued to vent his fury, feeling the same burn in his belly he had experienced with Asmodeus earlier.

As he raged, the inmates in the yard around them began to grow restless. Suspicious glances were shared accusingly, and even his father appeared to become agitated. A trio of large men broke away from a group, and made their way towards the table. Two of them sat down while the third stood nearby.

"This is our bench." He rumbled, looking down on Tyler.

"I was here first. There are other tables." Tyler responded in a low tone, glancing up at the man. Aidan's rage faded as he watched the situation.

"Are you too good to sit with us?" One of the other men asked, leaning forward.

"I like my peace and quiet."

"Well, we like this table."

"Get lost," Tyler responded, locking a steely gaze on them. Aidan recognized the expression all too well. It was the same look he always had right before he lost his temper.

The inmate behind Tyler placed his hands on his shoulders and pulled Tyler backwards off the bench; throwing him to the ground, the man moved to take Tyler's seat on the bench. Scrambling to his feet, Tyler lunged forward, and tackled the other man to the ground. The remaining two inmates rose, and jumped to the aid of their companion. Within an instant, the three were punching, and kicking Tyler viciously.

Aidan watched the scene with satisfaction. It seemed that justice was finally being done. All too often he had found himself on the receiving end of his father's temper. This time, it was his father who was experiencing what it was like to be bullied by larger men, and to feel weak under their power.

As he watched, he began to recall the times his father had taken his frustrations out on him, and his own helplessness. His father had once seemed large, and imposing to Aidan, but now he only seemed small and weak. In fact, Aidan now wondered if he had lost weight in the last couple weeks. How could this man have ever frightened him?

Gradually his anger faded, and he began to feel sorry for Tyler. Aidan looked around for guards to step in. Distantly, he could see them running towards the fight, but they seemed to be moving too slowly. For all his mistakes, his father didn't deserve the same treatment that he had inflicted on others so often. This was not justice, it was revenge. Aidan found himself feeling guilty for reveling in the violence.

"How do I stop this?" He said, looking urgently at Azriel for help.

"The same way you helped start it," Azriel said gently.

Aidan felt his panic rise when he couldn't remember how it had all started. Then he recalled his anger, and took a deep breath. He closed his eyes, and tried to will those around him to be calm. It was hard to focus on being calm amongst the chaos. Centering his attention on the birds that chirped in the distance, a sense of calm washed over him, and he was distantly aware of the fight ending.

The assault of his father slowed as the three men seemed to lose interest. They took a few steps back, their demeanor still aggressive, but somewhat calmer. The trio moved away from his father as they heard the shouted orders of the approaching guards. Two officers helped Tyler to his feet, and escorted him to the medical ward, while the other guards detained the three men. Opening his eyes, Aidan watched his father be escorted away.

"I am proud of you," Azriel said warmly, looking at Aidan with respect.

Aidan shifted uncomfortably, thrusting his hands into his pockets, and looking down. "I wanted them to hurt him."

"But you also showed mercy. We are all capable of evil, but it is our choices that make us good. Your anger did not blind you, and trick you into thinking that revenge is the same as justice. Rather you showed compassion for a person who has done you harm. This proves what I have always suspected about you." Azriel explained.

"And what is that?"

"That even though you share the same fury as Asmodeus, you are not like him. Asmodeus would have encouraged further violence, but you chose peace." Azriel said, still looking at him proudly.

"I felt bad for him," Aidan said, and shrugged awkwardly. "So is that what I was supposed to learn?"

"No, I am observing that you have proven yourself to be good. What you were meant to witness, is how our presence can influence events to unfold. Your anger was directed so powerfully towards your father that the other men felt resentful towards him. If they were to think about it, they may wonder what inspired such emotions so suddenly, but at the time they felt that it was natural to fight with him." Azriel said, beginning to walk through the courtyard.

"So we control what people do?" Aidan asked, thinking back to their conversation weeks earlier when Azriel had assured him it was not so.

"Not at all. On a subconscious level, humans can sense our presence, and respond emotionally to us. If we are angry, they will feel agitated, and may make choices accordingly. Similarly, if we are calm, we can inspire peace. But our presence does not negate their free will in choosing how to respond." To demonstrate, Azriel approached two men who appeared uneasy. His calm presence soothed them. "Understand?"

"Yes, but what does this have to do with the combat Asmodeus was teaching me."

"What were you using to fight each other with?"

"Anger," Aidan said, beginning to understand what Azriel was trying to show him. "So if we had been near anyone we could have influenced them?"

"Precisely, and this is why you are trained in our garden. The garden walls are sealed to contain our presence, so our influence does not extend beyond them. Most dwellings of our kind are designed in such a manner, because the longer we reside somewhere, the longer our influence lingers. Perhaps that is why the dwelling places of a Shade are often considered haunted by humans, while the Aduro's dwellings become sacred." Azriel said with an amused look. "But come, I have one more thing to show you."

≈≈≈≈≈≈≈≈

Azriel returned them to the garden, and motioned around them. "What do you notice about this place?"

Aidan looked around, trying to pick out what Azriel wished him to see. All around them flowers blossomed, and thrived in their wild environment. Despite having no gardener to care for them, the garden was pristine. As dusk approached, the garden was bathed in a warm glow making it even more beautiful.

"Flowers?" He said uncertainly.

"Yes, the garden is flourishing." Azriel turned, and led him to the portion of the garden where they had been training earlier. "And what do you see here?"

He immediately noticed that the grass where Asmodeus had pinned him had withered, and did not appear as healthy. Aidan frowned, and knelt down, touching the brown grass. "This is where Asmodeus had pinned me. The grass is dying."

"You can choose the mark you wish to make on the world. If it is anger, and hatred you wish to leave, this will be the result." Azriel nodded. "Asmodeus's anger caused this. In his rage, he draws life from the surrounding area. The fact that you attacked with anger only made it easier for him to do this. In fact, in a typical fight, he would have fed off your anger, and drawn the life from you."

Aidan stared numbly at the withered grass. "Why didn't he?"

"Because my presence keeps him from being truly evil, so he would not harm you. He is an extremely dark being, but not entirely evil. He is the dark, and I am the light, but together we achieve balance. It is the importance of this balance that you must learn today." Azriel took a deep breath, and then continued.

"Our world is about balance. If there are too many Shade, the world becomes a place full of despair and sickness. But alternatively light cannot exist without darkness. In combat, and all other things, we must strive for this balance as well. If two opponents only use darkness to fight, they will harm the world around them. This is why it is important to combat darkness with light."

"So because I fought with anger, does that make me a Shade?" Aidan frowned as he considered the idea.

"Not at all." Azriel chuckled in good nature. "Even an Aduro is capable of anger, Aidan. Anger often fuels passion, which prompts actions."

Aidan nodded, and Azriel regarded him with a kind expression. "But I think that is enough for one day. You have made wonderful progress, and deserve a break. Is there anything you wish to do?"

"I'd like to see Jazmine," Aidan answered.

Azriel nodded, unsurprised by the request. "Then perhaps there is one more lesson. To go there, recall a vivid memory of the place, and focus your mind on being there. To return, do the same."

Aidan grinned. "You mean I can teleport myself?"

"Yes, there is little need for walking in our world." He said with a wink. "Now off you go."

Azriel turned away, and crouched by the withered grass. Placing his hand on the grass, he closed his eyes, and slowly life returned to the withered area. Aidan lingered for a moment, watching his mentor work. Hoping that it would still be Azriel there when he returned, Aidan closed his eyes. He recalled the memory of a stealing a kiss in Jazmine's room, and then felt a slight tug as he vanished from the garden.

Fourteen...

"Do not dwell in the past, do not dream of the future,
concentrate the mind on the present moment."
– Buddha

Aidan opened his eyes and looked around the familiar surroundings of Jazmine's tidy room. Typically, she always had music playing but today her radio was silent. On her desk her math book was opened, with an empty notebook beside it. Even her bed remained unmade, which was unusual. Jazmine wasn't in her room, which made him wonder where she was, given that she was usually home at this time.

Intent on finding her, Aidan passed through the closed door, and began to wander the house. The home's layout was as familiar to him as his own house. In many ways, this was his second home, and he shared a strong bond with the family that resided here.

He paused in the hallway to look at the many family photos that hung on the walls. A pang of longing struck him as he looked at the photos where the parents laughed with their two daughters. The pictures displayed a timeline of the family, from marriage to the present day, and in each milestone, they all smiled at the camera. That was how a family was supposed to be. People you could depend on through difficult times.

Jazmine's parents had always been relaxed, and encouraged their children to express themselves. They had even allowed her to have a tattoo of music notes on her shoulder for her seventeenth birthday. It wasn't that they weren't firm parents, they managed to balance rules with self-expression. They had always amazed him with their diplomatic parenting.

Downstairs Aidan heard the front door open, and the muffled sound of conversation. Moving to the top of the stairs, he heard the sound of Jazmine's greeting, and her father's welcome.

"How is Aidan?" He asked, the concern evident in his voice.

"Still no improvement." She answered, with an exhausted sigh. It hurt to hear her so disheartened. She didn't sound like her normal cheerful self.

Aidan heard the old armchair creak, and he pictured her father embracing her as he spoke again. "Don't give up hope. Aidan is tough. He will pull through."

"Thanks, Dad," Jazmine answered, her voice sounding rough. "I'm going to shower, and then get some sleep. See you in the morning."

"Night sweetie." Her father replied.

Hearing Jazmine approach the stairs, Aidan retreated to her bedroom. He felt guilty for eavesdropping, but it wasn't like he could participate in the conversation. For a moment he stood in the middle of her room, feeling awkward. Finally, he sat on the bed, watching the door. Distantly he heard running water as the shower was started.

As he waited he spotted a picture of them together. The room was filled with so many fond memories of his time with her that he almost found it too difficult to stay. But his desire to see Jazmine was stronger, so he stayed where he was. Finally, he heard the shower turn off.

A few minutes later, the door opened, and Jazmine came in wearing her bathrobe. She closed the door behind her, and looked in her dresser for her pajamas. Aidan watched her sadly, missing her terribly now. He looked down at his hands as she took off the robe to change. Typically, he wasn't shy with her, but it felt wrong to watch her when she didn't know he was there. He kept his head down, intending to give her enough time to dress.

What he wouldn't give to be able to talk to her again. He had always taken things for granted with her. Their long conversations had always seemed like something he would never have to be without, but now here he was, sitting in her room, only steps away, and unable to talk to her. Aidan vowed never to take a conversation with her for granted.

Jazmine gave a small yelp as she heard his sigh, and spun around. "Aidan?" She exclaimed as she caught sight of him sitting on her bed.

Aidan sat up sharply, and looked at her with a stunned expression. "You can see me?" His mind was racing with excitement. He could have a small piece of home again. He recalled the night that he had visited with Azriel, and how she had responded to his voice while she had slept. He stood slowly, uncertain how to start explaining everything to her.

"How did you get here? I saw you at the hospital." She moved towards him to hug him before he could stop her. Jazmine's arms passed through him, and she muffled another cry of surprise. The color left her cheeks as she stepped back. "Are you -?" She broke off her sentence, afraid to finish.

"Dead? No, I'm still in the coma as far as I know." He said quickly to reassure her, although he realized his words would probably be more confusing than reassuring.

From the bottom of the stairs, Jazmine's dad called up, distracting them both for a moment. "Honey, are you okay? We thought we heard you yell?"

"Yea Dad, it was just a spider. I'm fine." Jazmine called back, as she ducked her head out into the hallway.

"Do you need me to come kill it?" He called, starting up the stairs.

"No, I got it." She called back hastily. "Night."

Closing the door again, Jazmine sank heavily into her desk chair. She echoed his sigh, clearly concerned. "For a second I thought you might have been better..." She whispered, looking across the room at him, and trying to hide her disappointment.

"Jazz, you are taking this pretty well. Aren't you freaked out at all?" Aidan said, watching her curiously. He would not have been so composed in her situation.

It was Jazmine's turn to look uncomfortable as she stared down at her hands. "I've never told anyone before, but sometimes I catch glimpses of things. Movement out of the corner of my eye, whispers, and stuff like that. Most of the time I thought I imagined it. But unless I'm dreaming right now, I'd say I wasn't."

"Why didn't you ever tell me?"

"That I thought I could see ghosts? That's not exactly something you bring up on a date. I thought you would think I was crazy. I've never even told my parents." She said defensively. Her color returned as she blushed.

"Fair enough." He said, recalling Azriel's warnings. "I'm glad you can. I've missed you. I have wanted to talk to you so much." He said, giving her a warm smile.

"I'm glad you are here too. I've been very worried. But you could do some explaining," She admitted, returning the smile with a tentative one. "Like how you are here exactly."

"It's been a crazy couple of days. There's a lot to explain, and I still don't understand all of it myself." He admitted.

"Aidan, it's been almost two weeks." She said, frowning.

"Has it been that long? I didn't notice that much time had gone by." He said, sitting down slowly on the bed again. "I guess I've been so busy with training."

"Training?"

Aidan took a deep breath, wondering how to explain everything that had happened. "There's this whole world that exists alongside ours, Jazmine." He began. "There are all these...ghosts, and they are at war with each other." Aidan paused for a moment, trying to think of the best way to describe this new realm. Calling them ghosts seemed inadequate, but it was the closest description available.

"And you are training for this war?" Jazmine asked. "Why would you even get involved?"

"Well, Gabrielle needs my help," Aidan answered, reddening slightly as he thought of Gabrielle in Jazmine's presence. When Jazmine arched a brow quizzically, he quickly explained. "She's the leader of the Aduro, the ghosts that are like angels. She said she could send me home once I've helped her. Someone, probably a Shade, is blocking her powers, so he needs to be taken care of first." The words tumbled out in a rush.

Jazmine listened in silence as he explained, worry lines creasing her forehead as her brow furrowed. "And you think you can do what she needs you to do?"

"She seems to think so," Aidan answered.

"Is she the one training you?"

"No, she's assigned Asmodeus and Azriel to teach me." He grimly explained his first meeting with Asmodeus, and the training he had received with him.

"He sounds awful." Jazz said, frowning as she listened to his account. "And he is supposed to be teaching you?"

"He isn't a very good teacher because he is too impatient, but I guess I am stuck with him. I can see why Gabrielle wants Asmodeus to teach me, though. He is pretty good at fighting, but I still prefer working with Azriel."

"What is this Azriel like?"

"He's completely different from Asmodeus. He's calm and patient. I think he cares about me. Half the time Asmodeus seems as likely to kill me, as help me." He admitted bleakly.

"Can't you stay with Azriel?"

"That's the thing; they are the same person. So to be around one, I have to be around the other. It's a split personality thing."

Jazmine frowned, and arched a brow skeptically. "That sounds dysfunctional."

Aidan laughed, knowing she had described the situation perfectly. "No kidding. I need all the help I can get, so I can't be picky. Besides, I don't think Gabrielle has anyone else who can train me for what I am supposed to do. She's convinced that Asmodeus is the best one for the job."

"But what if you can't do what Gabrielle needs you to do? What if something happens to you?"

Aidan looked away from Jazz, reluctant to face what he had been avoiding. "I guess… I would stay in the coma or die." He said slowly, finally admitting that there was a possibility of death to himself.

Jazmine was silent for a few moments as she took in the news then finally spoke. "But that won't happen." Jazz said with conviction.

"No. I'm doing everything I can so it won't." He assured her. Aidan moved to hug her, but stopped himself, recalling that he wouldn't be able to touch her. He frowned. He thought visiting Jazz would help him forget everything for a moment. Instead, the visit had made everything seem even more bleak.

Jazz stared at him for a long moment, then sighed, and looked down. "Is there anything I can do to help?"

"Keep an eye on my Mom, and look after her if anything happens to me." He said.

"Nothing will happen to you, but I'll watch out for her."

"Thanks, Jazz." He glanced at the time. "Shouldn't you be sleeping? It's late."

Jazz tried to lighten up the mood. "I was going to sleep, but I got distracted by the ghost of my boyfriend appearing in my bedroom." She forced a laugh, trying to liven them both up.

"Maybe I should go, and let you rest. Azriel is probably wondering where I am anyway." Aidan said reluctantly, appreciative of her humor, but not finding it terribly effective.

"Why don't you stay here?" She offered. "It's not like we would be breaking any rules since my parents can't see you." Jazz said, still trying to cheer him up.

"I don't need to sleep. I guess that's why time has felt so different for me." He said.

"Oh. Well, can you stay a while longer? Just until I fall asleep?" She said, not wanting him to go yet.

"Of course." He answered.

Jazz climbed into bed, pulling the blankets up. Nestling under the covers, she looked up at him. "You'll visit me again, won't you?"

"As much as I can." He promised in a whisper as he lay down beside her. "Sweet dreams, Jazz."

"Night, Aidan. I'm glad I can see you." She whispered into the darkness after she turned out the light.

Aidan lay perfectly still, waiting for her to drift into slumber. For a moment he thought she had, when she whispered four words that only furthered his resolve to return home to her.

"I love you, Aidan." Gradually her breathing slowed as she drifted off. Aidan lingered as he couldn't bring himself to leave as she slept, studying her peaceful expression. It wasn't until the first light of dawn started to brighten the room that he finally returned to Azriel's garden.

Fifteen...

"Hope is like the sun, which as we journey towards it,
casts the shadow of our burden behind us."
– Samuel Smiles

Golden light crept into the garden as dawn arrived. Azriel walked through the garden, tending to any flowers which threatened to succumb to disease or other ailments. He enjoyed the peace of caring for the garden. It provided him with times of solitude as Asmodeus refused to make an appearance there, save for his lessons with Aidan.

He hummed softly to himself as he worked. "Welcome back. I trust you had a good visit." Azriel did not need to turn to know that Aidan had returned from his visit with Jazmine. Aidan's excitement brought palatable energy to the air.

"She can see me, Azriel." He announced, clearly thrilled by the news.

"I cannot say I am surprised, only apprehensive, due to the concerns I have already expressed," Azriel said, seating himself on the stone bench. It was his favorite spot, as the sun often warmed the stone throughout the morning.

"I know you said she might be capable of seeing me, but she didn't see me at first. Then suddenly she could see, and hear me. It was great!" He said, still brimming with excitement.

"I imagine it was her gift to see our realm along with your desire to see her, that made it possible," Azriel said, answering the question that Aidan had yet to ask. "And how did she react?"

"Better than I expected," Aidan admitted. "She was freaked out at first, but she calmed down pretty quick. Apparently, she's caught glimpses of things her whole life, and never told anyone."

"And is she going to say anything to anyone now?"

"I don't think so. She hasn't told anyone about what she had seen before. I doubt she would now."

"That is probably for the best," Azriel advised. "But I'm glad you could see her as you desired. Hopefully, you are ready to renew your training now that you have rested, and had some time to yourself." He did not want to detract from Aidan's happiness, but he was aware of the pressing timeline of the boy's training. He imagined that his brief contact with home would only intensify his determination.

Aidan nodded reluctantly. "Will Asmodeus be teaching me?"

"No, we thought it would be best that I provide this lesson. It is not combat training, so my instruction will be adequate. In fact, my healing abilities are better than Asmodeus's, which will serve as the foundation for the task at hand."

"Okay," Aidan said, clearly pleased that he would not have to deal with Asmodeus. "I like that idea better."

Azriel nodded, understanding what he meant. "I thought that would be the case. Sit with me, and our lesson will begin."

After Aidan had seated himself, Azriel formed a small dagger in his hand. "The ultimate goal is to learn to absorb energy from your surroundings. First, we will begin with learning how to use your own energy to heal. Once you have mastered that, it will be easier to draw energy from others."

With his lesson plan outlined, Azriel rolled up his sleeve, and placed the blade against his forearm. He carefully drew a long thin line into his skin. Instead of blood, light shone out of the wound. Aidan stared at the light, still unaccustomed to the sight. The bloodless existence in this realm was unsettling to observe.

"Place your hand over the wound," Azriel said, and then continued his instructions as Aidan did so. "It often helps to visualize the wound closing. As you do so, imagine that it is your will, and energy that is stitching the wound closed."

Azriel watched as Aidan focused on his appointed task. A slight smile crept onto his expression as he observed his pupil make his first attempts. He was a dedicated student, a trait that inspired Azriel's confidence that he would succeed at Gabrielle's task. He intended to prepare Aidan as thoroughly as possible for whatever lay ahead. Aidan continuously surprised him with his aptitude for adjusting to the rules of their realm, and learning these otherwise foreign concepts.

His gaze shifted to the cut on his arm, and watched for any change. It was deep enough that it would not close on its own, but shallow enough not to drain his strength quickly.

Gradually he became aware of a slight tingle around the cut. He nodded in approval, knowing that it was as a result of Aidan's efforts. Slowly the skin came together, sealing the light away. He could feel the edges bind together, and nodded approvingly as he felt his lost energy return. When the wound healed flawlessly Aidan removed his hand.

"Good. How was that?"

"Easier than I thought." Aidan responded, causing Azriel to chuckle. "Although somewhat tiring."

"That is to be expected. To heal, you must use your own energy to replenish your patient's lost resources. So be careful that you do not try to heal a wound that is beyond the limits of your energy reserve." He cautioned. "But Gabrielle was right about you being powerful. You adapt so easily to our world, almost like it is natural for you to be here."

"Asmodeus does not seem to agree with you," Aidan said doubtfully.

Now Azriel laughed in good humor. "Asmodeus would never admit to agreeing with us about anything. Besides, you shouldn't take his actions or words personally. He is difficult to get along with at the best of times. I am often glad that I do not have to interact with him, and only catch glimpses of his doings."

"You don't know what he does?"

"No," Azriel admitted. "I suppose it is like I am sleeping when he takes over. At times I can recall what he has done, but usually, it is like a vague dream. Occasionally we communicate, but typically we don't bother."

"Why is that?"

"We don't care for one another, to be honest. He thinks I am weak, and treats me with disdain. I find him rash, and overly harsh. There are many things he has done that I find distasteful, but, he does have the power to carry out tasks that I would not be able to do. I suppose that is why Gabrielle tolerates him. He is a powerful soldier, even if a rather insubordinate one." As Azriel spoke of his counterpart, he gave a disappointed sigh.

Often, Azriel found himself wondering how he could share a soul with a personality so different. Despite knowing how it had happened, he often found the reality of it difficult. It was a complicated existence.

"But let us return to your lesson, enough talk of Asmodeus." He said, not wishing to linger on something he could not change. "You mastered healing easily enough, so now we will attempt to do the opposite. Instead of giving your energy to me, use the same method to draw energy from me instead. For now, physical contact is required, so keep that in mind."

Aidan nodded, and placed his hand back on Azriel's forearm. He was about to proceed when he hesitated. "I won't hurt you, will I?"

"You will not draw enough energy from me to do lasting harm. If you begin to take too much, I will break the contact. Do not worry; you will not harm me. Continue." He said encouragingly.

He waited patiently as Aidan took a deep breath, and then closed his eyes to concentrate. For a long time, Azriel sat without feeling anything. Finally, he felt his limbs become heavy, and he knew Aidan had been successful. He allowed Aidan to continue to take a small portion of his energy before pulling his arm away.

"Excellent. How do you feel now?"

"Stronger," Aidan said, sitting straighter.

Azriel nodded. "The exchange of energy is how we become weaker or stronger. If you absorb enough energy from another soul, you will eventually end their existence."

"You can kill someone like this?" Aidan was alarmed. "And you let me do that to you?"

"Yes, because I have faith that you would not wish to harm me, and therefore instinctively would have stopped yourself. But it is important that you know what can happen if you do go too far."

"I'll make sure I don't." He said shakily. "Is that what Asmodeus did to the Shade?"

"Most likely. It is how he remains so powerful. He has no qualms about destroying Shades who challenge him. Gabrielle frequently uses him as her bounty hunter to remove Shades who are too much of a threat."

"Aren't you equally as powerful than if you are the same soul?" Aidan asked.

"Yes, but my talents are in other areas. Gabrielle has a use for both of us, but in different ways. I think she also tolerates Asmodeus because of my presence."

"So why does your power feel so much different than his?"

"I imagine you can figure out the answer to that question yourself."

Aidan thought for a moment, and then answered. "Because you are light, and he is dark?"

"Very good. Our power is a representation of ourselves, and our personalities. Much of what you are sensing is the emotions which fuel our power. Asmodeus lashes out with rage, and bitterness when he makes contact. I am gentler, and that is what you sense in my company."

Aidan nodded, knowing that was why he preferred to be around Azriel.

"Our energy can even leave a mark which allows you to detect who left it. Think of it as a type of signature. It can be difficult to sense, however, especially if efforts were taken to conceal the mark."

Aidan nodded again, and Azriel smiled warmly. He could not deny that he was fond of Aidan. "Shall we continue practicing?"

Sixteen...

"The angel of death has been abroad throughout the land, you may almost hear the beating of his wings."
– John Bright

As usual, the hospital was busy. Illness and disease never took a rest, and it was the responsibility of the nurses to help care for the patients. Jaclyn, a transfer from another hospital, had started on the ward a few months ago. She was a veteran nurse who often thought that her years of experience helped her predict the odds of her patients making a recovery. She, unfortunately, was seldom wrong.

During her recent shift, there was one patient who she did not have a good feeling about; Aidan, had remained in a coma for nearly three weeks. Never a good sign. His coma, had been brought on by head trauma after domestic violence, a kinder way to say abuse.

She had heard that his father had been arrested, but she wondered how long the system would be able to keep him locked up. What sort of life would Aidan be returning to if he did wake up? It was that thought that made her question her job. Even if he could make it through the coma without permanent damage, what would stop this from happening again?

Pondering these questions once again, Jaclyn wheeled her cart into Aidan's room. Methodically she began to check his vital signs, and replace his IV bag. She was about to leave when her hand passed over the syringe she had filled with poison and tucked into her cart.

Wouldn't it be better to end his suffering?

The voice of reassurance whispered in her mind. She had had such thoughts before, but never acted upon them. Yet this time, she found herself thinking that a peaceful death would be kinder for this particular patient.

It would be kinder. The voice whispered in her mind again.

His health did seem to be declining naturally. At some point he might stop breathing on his own and they would have to bring in life support machines. Maybe it would save his poor mother from having to make the choice of when her son dies. No parent should ever have to make that decision.

Somberly, she once again gave in to the temptation. This was not her first dose of poison for him, but each injection made her question herself anew. Yet each time the decision was the same.

Steeling her nerve, she grasped the syringe, and injected it into his IV. It was a slow acting poison so his passing would not look suspicious. As much as she wanted to help him, she didn't want to be caught for something that she would never do again. With the poison administered, she placed the needle in the sharps receptacle, and turned back to her cart.

As she turned, she noticed a girl watching her from the doorway. Her heart skipped a beat, and she jumped.

"Oh my, you surprised me." She said, trying to laugh off the possibility that she had been caught.

"Oh sorry, I'm Jazz. How is Aidan doing?" The girl asked, glancing towards Aidan's motionless body.

"He seems to be doing well. I'm sure the doctor will be by at some point if you'd like to speak with him." Jaclyn offered helpfully.

"Okay, thanks." Jazz said, and took a seat by Aidan's bed.

As quickly as possible, Jaclyn hurried from the room. She glanced over her shoulder at Jazmine, but the girl didn't seem suspicious so gradually she relaxed. As Jaclyn carried on with her rounds, the voice continued to reassure her that she had done the right thing.

≈≈≈≈≈≈≈≈≈

Jazmine had skipped last period to arrive as visiting hours began at the hospital. Typically, she never skipped classes, but she figured her parents wouldn't mind under the circumstances. Even though she was in her final year at school, they didn't hound her to keep up with her school work. She couldn't focus on the material anyway. Moreover, who could expect her to be focused?

It had been days since she had seen Aidan in her room, and she felt desperate to see him again. Somehow she doubted that he would linger by his motionless body, but she hoped regardless. It was that dim hope that had brought her to the hospital. Even if she could not speak with him, at least she could be by his side.

Yet Jazmine could not quiet the lingering doubt that Aidan's visit had been a dream. Naturally, she had been exhausted and stressed. Perhaps her subconscious had fulfilled her wish to speak to him again with a dream? But she had always had strange glimpses in the past. Could it be possible that it hadn't been a dream?

Waiting for the elevator to arrive, she suppressed an unhappy sigh. If only she had some way to know if it had been real or not. His visit was still vivid in her mind, and the details of their conversation weren't fading like the details of most dreams did. But the only sure way would be to have another visit, and that was beyond her control. She hated doubting herself, but didn't feel entirely confident about what she had seen either.

Stepping out of the elevator, Jazmine made her way through the hallway to Aidan's room. She stopped at the threshold as she caught a glimpse of two figures in the room. The first was a nurse, bent over Aidan as she checked his vitals, and injected some medicine into his IV. The second figure stood behind the woman watching her work intently. As Jazz tried to focus on the figure's features, her eyes blurred like she was looking through a haze.

Jazmine blinked, and the man was gone. She frowned, and shook her head. Was the stress getting to her more than she thought? But then if she had seen Aidan, it was possible. As she tried to remember what the man had looked like, she realized she couldn't quite recall. He had been dressed oddly, and she knew he was an older man, but could not picture his face now that he had vanished.

Trying to put the figure out of her mind, Jazmine watched the nurse work for a moment. The nurse's behavior puzzled her. It seemed that she was nervous, but Jazz couldn't figure out why. Jazz apologized when the nurse seemed startled when she turned around.

"Oh sorry, I'm Jazz. How is Aidan doing?" Jazz asked. She listened to the nurse's reply about the doctor being in shortly, and then nodded. "Thanks." She said, but the nurse had already hurried out of the room. Must be a busy day, Jazmine thought to herself.

Going to Aidan's bedside, she took a seat in the metal chair. She took hold of his hand, and studied his expression, hoping for some change. Jazz finally sighed, unable to deny her confusion any longer.

"Aidan, I wish I knew if the other night had been real." She said, squeezing his hand gently. "I want to believe it was, but I haven't seen you in days. You have to give me a sign that I'm not crazy." She laughed awkwardly to herself, feeling foolish, but trying to reassure herself with humor.

For a long time, she sat with him. She talked about anything that came to mind. Just like in the movies, the doctors had told them that hearing familiar voices helped coma patients. The thought did provide comfort, and helped her to feel less awkward while carrying on a one-sided conversation.

After a while, a knock at the door interrupted her monologue. Turning, she gave a slight wave as she saw Doctor Briggs. "Hey, Doc."

"Good afternoon, Jazmine. How are you today?" He responded.

"I'm okay."

"You seem tired. Have you been taking care of yourself?" The doctor asked.

"I've been trying to."

"Good, he wouldn't want you making yourself sick." He said kindly.

"How is he doing? Any change?"

The doctor frowned slightly. "Unfortunately, his vitals are weakening, which concerns me. His brain activity is still promising, but his vitals are not where I would like them to be."

"What does that mean long term?"

"It could be nothing. He may still improve. Either way, we will continue to monitor him closely." The doctor paused for a moment. He did not like to lessen a family's hopes, but he found that being realistic helped to prepare them. "There is one thing to keep in mind. The longer he is in a coma, the greater the risk there is for a lingering disability after he wakes up."

Jazz nodded slightly. "I've been doing some research." It helped her feel more in control, or at least more knowledgeable. "I won't give up on him yet."

"Good, he needs encouragement. Did you have any questions about your anything you've found?" When Jazz shook her head, the doctor continued. "When Mrs. Matheson arrives, I will give her the same report. I will have a nurse page me when she gets here." Doctor Briggs said.

"Thanks." Jazz said. She watched the doctor leave, and then turned back to Aidan. Resting her elbow on the bed, she held her head in her hand. The doctor's visit left her feeling less hopeful than before.

"Aidan, you better wake up." She whispered to him. "Keep fighting."

Seventeen...

"For success, attitude is equally as important as ability."
– Walter Scott

Aidan countered Asmodeus's blow with a quick parry, and dodged the next attack with lithe speed. He was so concentrated on the sparring that he did not spare a thought to plan his next move or even to congratulate himself on his present success. Each move was instinctual, and unhindered by thoughts of what he might be doing wrong.

A steady schedule of sparring sessions had provided him with a wide repertoire of tactics to use during the matches. It had taken quite a while, but gradually he began to withstand Asmodeus's assaults for longer periods of time. Occasionally Aidan had even managed to land a blow or two. He no longer spent all his time defending himself; rather he was able to spend an equal amount of time attacking in turn.

Their present sparring session found him in good form. He reacted quickly to each attack Asmodeus attempted, preventing him from landing any strikes. In one hand he held a shield, and in the other, he held his single-handed sword. The weapons suited him perfectly since he could block attacks, and counter quickly with the sword. As usual, Asmodeus fought ruthlessly with his broadsword, having no need for a shield since he blocked effectively with his blade.

Asmodeus had been unusually quiet during their recent sparring sessions. His lack of taunting was the only compliment Aidan needed. He had accepted that he would hear no kind words from Asmodeus, and contented himself with the knowledge that no insults meant he was improving.

Asmodeus brought his sword down for another heavy blow. Bringing his shield up, Aidan felt the blade glance off. With the impact, he felt a surge of anger from Asmodeus, but his shield held strong. Aidan was not goaded into feeling angry, he held firmly to the compassion which he had used to create his weapons.

Aidan had made many attempts at crafting a weapon that could withstand Asmodeus's fury. The only thing Asmodeus's rage could not devour was the strong sense of compassion Aidan had discovered during his visit with his Father. The newfound compassion seemed to confound Asmodeus. Rage could not harm him when he had empathy for Asmodeus's suffering.

For a moment Aidan was distracted by his thoughts, and Asmodeus took advantage of the opening. He brought his sword forward, and broke through Aidan's defenses. Asmodeus stopped the blade above Aidan's heart. Aidan lifted his hands, and gave a slight nod to acknowledge that he had been defeated.

"Again," Asmodeus commanded, providing no suggestion for improvement, but not rebuking Aidan for his slip in attention.

Aidan took a few steps back, and prepared himself for the next round of attacks. He took the moment to strengthen his shield with more energy. He watched Asmodeus carefully, noticing that for the first time he showed some signs of tiring. Asmodeus didn't launch immediately into another fight, but took a moment to gather himself. The sign gave Aidan hope that he might be able to best Asmodeus soon.

Aidan was about to make the first move when Asmodeus put up his hand to halt the session. He looked towards the garden gate, and Aidan followed his gaze to where Zacharias stood.

"Zacharias, what are you doing here?" Asmodeus asked coolly.

"Gabrielle sent me to observe how Aidan's training has progressed."

"Does she not trust my judgment regarding his readiness?"

Zacharias laughed at his question. "Asmodeus, she questions your judgment daily. However, in this particular case, she knows you are overly critical. Hence my presence today to ensure that you are not holding him back unnecessarily."

Asmodeus grunted in response, shooting him an irritated glare. "Just stay quiet. I don't need you distracting him."

Aidan glanced between the two men. He was not surprised to sense Asmodeus's disdain for Zacharias. However, he was surprised that Asmodeus did not respond with a sharper remark. It was not like him to hold his tongue, and it made Aidan wonder about the shift in his behavior.

Zacharias moved to a corner of the garden where he would be out of the way. Conscious of Zacharias's eyes on him, Aidan prepared himself for another match. He tried to ignore the possible implications of the sparring match. If he performed well, Zacharias might deem him ready, which meant he was another step closer to going home.

Asmodeus attacked with new ferocity, as if determined to prove that his student had not surpassed him. He made a rash lunge, a mistake that he had scolded Aidan for many times during their early sessions. Aidan sidestepped the attack nimbly, and brought his shield up in anticipation of a deceptive trick. He was used to fighting a calculating opponent, not the careless one he fought now.

He did not let the change in Asmodeus distract him. Aidan remained focused, suspicious that Asmodeus was employing a new ruse to lower his guard. He countered each blow calmly, and made his own strategic attacks. Gradually he gained ground as Asmodeus began to weaken and slow. Determined not to become overly-confident, Aidan paid careful attention to what he was doing, still expecting a trick.

The session dragged on. Asmodeus was still a formidable opponent, but lacked his usual flair. Aidan remained wary, despite being aware of what winning the match might mean.

Aidan was beginning to tire as well when he finally saw an opening in Asmodeus's defense. He had shifted his weight a little too far, and lowered his sword a bit too low. Quickly Aidan seized the opportunity. He slammed his shield into Asmodeus. Stumbling, Asmodeus tried to recover his balance, but failed. He fell back. With his opponent down, Aidan brought his sword forward, and rested it against Asmodeus's neck. Feeling the steel against his skin, Asmodeus nodded in submission.

Aidan withdrew his sword, and gave a respectful nod to Asmodeus. Extending his hand out to help pull him to his feet. He felt some pride for his accomplishment, but was also hesitant about the victory. It had felt too easy compared to his other matches with Asmodeus. He knew he had improved greatly, but Asmodeus had always been far superior.

Meanwhile, Zacharias clapped loudly, smirking at Asmodeus as he approached them. "Well done, Aidan! I have never seen anyone best Asmodeus."

"Yes, congratulations," Asmodeus said, his words uncharacteristically void of any snide remarks.

"Thanks," Aidan said awkwardly. He watched Asmodeus carefully, uneasy with the sudden change in him. Something wasn't right, but he didn't question the change in front of Zacharias.

"You are ready to see Gabrielle. She will be very pleased with your progress." Zacharias said happily. "Shall we go now?"

"I guess so," Aidan answered, still hesitating as he watched Asmodeus, and his curious behavior. "Are you coming?"

"Gabrielle has instructed that you come alone," Zacharias interjected quickly, clearly pleased to exclude Asmodeus.

"Go on," Asmodeus answered in his typical snide tone. "I would prefer being in my own company for a while."

Strangely reassured by the familiar snide tone, Aidan nodded to Zacharias. "Let's go."

~~~~~~~~~~

Zacharias delivered him to the cathedral as soon as the words had left his mouth. Accustomed to teleporting now Aidan looked around calmly, only surprised by Zacharias's eagerness to bring him to Gabrielle.

Aidan climbed the spiraling staircase slowly, recalling the last time he had been here. It had only been a couple of weeks according to Jazmine, but it felt much longer to him. Time moved so differently in this world with no requirements for food or sleep. His time had been filled with lessons from Asmodeus and Azriel.

Night and day helped to mark the passing of time, but his body took little notice. In fact, he had only grown stronger in his time here. It was strange to think that not so long ago, he had understood nothing of this world, and now he functioned comfortably here. He was reluctant to admit to himself that in some ways he felt more at home.

It made him question what Azriel had said days before. Did he belong in this world? He seemed to adjust so easily, and learn so quickly. That was not something he had experienced in his world. If it hadn't been for

Jazmine and his Mom, he might have considered staying. His two ties to the human realm wouldn't allow him to consider the thought for more than a second.

As he reached the top of the stairs, Aidan put his thoughts aside. With any luck, he would be home soon, and this place would be a distant memory. Hopefully, Gabrielle would have good news for him. Stepping into the bell tower, he spotted her standing by the window watching the street below.

"Hello, Gabrielle." He said politely.

"Good morning, Aidan. It is lovely to see you again," She said in a cheerful voice, as she turned to face him. "You look well," Gabrielle said as she crossed the room, and embraced him.

As before, Aidan couldn't help but be struck by how attractive she was. Strange how his memory of her didn't do her justice. "Thank you. You look as beautiful as ever." He said, no longer blushing as he paid her the compliment.

"You flatter me." She answered warmly, and studied him for a moment. "You have changed since our last meeting. You have grown stronger than I even expected in this amount of time."

Aidan bowed his head slightly in acknowledgement. "I have been motivated by your promise to help me get home." He answered.

"You mean you don't wish to remain here with me? You have adapted so quickly, and could become so powerful here." Gabrielle said, her charming smile fading in confusion.

"I wish to return to my world. I have family members who are missing me." Aidan answered calmly, feeling a pang of loneliness as he thought of them.

Aidan was reminded of his earlier thoughts, and frowned. How could she have known his thoughts: unless her influence had guided them? Resentfully he shielded his mind, not willing to have her tamper with his mind again. As he did so, he could feel Gabrielle's influence testing the strength of his defenses.

"Do you not trust me?" Gabrielle said as she sensed the sudden barrier between them. She touched his cheek tenderly, trying to reassure him.

"I trust you, but Asmodeus taught me to keep a vigilant guard. He would be disappointed to know that I had failed." Aidan lied. Asmodeus had never instructed him to do so, but he could imagine that Asmodeus would encourage such paranoid precautions.

Gabrielle nodded, and seemed reassured. "You have been well trained. Although you will find no unfriendly influences here." She was silent for a moment, and then spoke again. "Then let us see about returning you home."

Gabrielle retreated a few steps. "But first, a test to prove your readiness." Two hilts shimmered to life in her hands and the twin blades extended into curved short swords. The blade edges shimmered with hints of gold and silver. The weapons were delicate, and beautiful like her.

Gabrielle watched him for a moment. "You should form your weapons if you intend to prove your skill," She advised. "We will spar, and I will judge your ability."

He hesitated for a moment, trying to gauge her skill before they began. Asmodeus has never mentioned if she was a skilled fighter, but he suspected she must be to lead the Aduro.

"Go on." She said encouragingly, although there was a note of command in her deceptively polite tone.

Aidan formed his own weapons carefully, ignoring the nervousness that threatened to overtake him. He suspected that the coming moments would define how quickly he would be able to return home. He constructed them primarily with compassion, but laced them with his eagerness to see Jazmine as well.

He took his stance, studying Gabrielle, and the position which she took. She looked so relaxed that Aidan was caught by surprise when she made the first move. Even her fighting style was graceful, like everything else about her. Sparring with her felt like a beautiful dance, despite his less graceful movements.

Aidan was reluctant to attack her, so he took a defensive role instead. She showed him no mercy, but he found that he could keep up with her attacks. Even as their weapons struck he was not weakened, proving that he was an equal match for her.

"Do not hold back, Aidan. I must see your true abilities to know if you are ready." Gabrielle advised after he blocked another of her strikes.

Aidan acknowledged her instructions by countering with an attack of his own. He dropped to one knee, and brought his shield up to block her sword while hiding the movement of his own hand. Bringing his sword forward, he moved to strike Gabrielle's leg. Her second sword blocked his, however. Quickly he rolled away as she brought her other sword forward. Recovering his composure nimbly, he regained his footing as he came out of the roll.

His mistake almost cost him the match, and he cursed himself for forgetting her second blade. He had gotten far too accustomed to fighting Asmodeus, and his single sword. Aidan wouldn't allow himself to make the same mistake twice.

He launched into a new round of attacks with more care and attention. Tirelessly the pair danced, and wove around one another. Neither gained the upper hand as they moved around the bell tower in unison.

Aidan watched carefully for an opening, trying to find her weakness. Her twin blades provided an effective defense, and a dangerous offence as he had to keep track of both blades. He played it cautious, biding his time for a moment when she would become careless. If Asmodeus had taught him one thing, it was patience. He had also picked up many of Asmodeus's crafty techniques, mostly through having fallen victim to them himself.

Aidan continued to hold his own in the match, while he searched for a way to gain the upper hand. They could not maintain this forever, one of them would eventually make a mistake, and Aidan was determined that it would not be him.

He saw Gabrielle's grip weaken as her sword glanced off his shield. Using the shield, he knocked her sword out of her hand, and saw it vanish as it fell from her grip. Before she could bring up the second blade to block, he brought the flat side of his sword against her collarbone.

Gabrielle signaled her surrender as she felt the cool touch of the weapon on her skin. She lifted her hands, and allowed her other sword to vanish. Aidan lowered his hand as his sword disappeared as well.

"Well done Aidan! You are truly ready." Gabrielle exclaimed proudly as she embraced him in a hug.

Aidan returned the hug slowly, his thoughts already jumping ahead. He had won against Gabrielle. If he could win against her, he could win against whoever was keeping him trapped here. It was only a matter of time before he was home again with Jazmine and his Mom. He couldn't stop grinning at the thought.

"So what is next? What is this task you mentioned?" Aidan asked.

"To answer that, I think we need to visit your body," Gabrielle said. "Zacharias will accompany us, as he has some answers to provide as well." Zacharias appeared as he was summoned, and Gabrielle whisked them away.

Eighteen...

"Fidelity – a virtue peculiar to those who are
about to be betrayed."
– Ambrose Bierce

The trio appeared in at the foot of Aidan's hospital bed. Aidan looked at the motionless body lying there. He knew he was looking at himself, yet he felt no lingering connection to his body. He did not feel the same pull that he had experienced the first day he had been here. Aidan glanced at the monitors, which still beeped and displayed his vitals. He wished he knew what the numbers meant.

"It must be strange to see yourself like this," Gabrielle said gently.

"Yeah, it is," Aidan admitted. "So why are we here? I thought we had to go deal with whoever is keeping me from returning to my body?"

"I thought this would be easier to explain if we were here."

"Okay," Aidan answered, and waited for her explanation.

"Do you know anything about how to pass your energy into objects?" Gabrielle asked, and when Aidan nodded, she continued. "Good. This is how you should be able to return to your body. Indulge me, and try now."

Aidan moved around to stand beside the bed. He studied himself, looking for some sign that he was still attached to his body. The bruise that had discolored his features had faded, and even the cut on his temple was only a faint scar. It seemed that even without his soul, his body still functioned to some degree.

Bringing his hand forward, he touched his skin lightly. He was surprised that he could make physical contact with his own body. He recalled how he had been unable to touch Jazmine. As he made contact, his finger twitched. The heart monitor numbers recorded a slight increase. It seemed that he did maintain some connection to his after all. Encouraged now, he closed his eyes to concentrate.

He focused on passing his energy to his own body. He hoped desperately that it would be as easy as this to return home. However, Aidan found that no amount of focus would return his soul to his body. A barrier still remained between them. Determined to break down the wall, he tried again with aggressive force. However, his attempts were met with steadfast resistance.

"Don't exhaust yourself. You are being kept from your body. Only the one who made the barrier can remove it." Gabrielle explained, gently taking his hand, and breaking his contact.

"So who is this mystery figure who is keeping me here?" Aidan asked, feeling his anger begin to stir. "I can't wait to meet them." He growled, his frustration growing.

"You already have," Gabrielle said, watching his reaction carefully. Aidan's eyes flicked towards Zacharias and Gabrielle shook her head. "No, it is not Zacharias. It is Asmodeus who keeps you here."

Aidan stared at her for a moment, trying to come to terms with what she had said. "Asmodeus?" He said skeptically. "But why would he keep me here? He hates me."

"Let us consider for a moment. Asmodeus is not a friend to you, but he knows your potential. If he can keep you here, he knows I would prefer to no longer call upon his services, but to call on you instead."

"But he was at my house, and at the hospital when I got there," Aidan said, trying to make sense of the timeline.

"And you think that is a coincidence? He built the wall before he met you, and then had the nerve to bring you to me." Gabrielle shook her head as she thought of Asmodeus. "He is a bold one."

"So why would you have him train me knowing what he did?"

"Who better to learn from than the one whom you must defeat?" She answered with a crafty expression. "He thought he was training his replacement, but he has given you the skills you need to defeat him, and return home."

"Smart," Aidan commented grimly. "But why was he at my house?"

"I suspect that is my fault," Gabrielle said, her expression contrite. "I confided in him about my vision of you."

"Gabrielle suspected Asmodeus would attempt some foul play, so she sent me to watch over you," Zacharias interjected. "I misjudged the power of

Asmodeus's influence, however, and I could not prevent the fight which he set in motion."

"But why would he come after me, though?"

"He knew I saw great potential in you. I did not lie when I said that it was your fate to be here, but that time was not supposed to be until your natural death. Asmodeus has grown tired of being under my command, and decided to speed your arrival. He wishes to be released from my service." Gabrielle explained.

"So he wants to keep me here?"

"Yes, he plans to trap you here until your body perishes for lack of a soul," Gabrielle said, frowning.

"So how I can go home?" He asked.

"Asmodeus must die."

A heavy silence fell over the room after Gabrielle's words. Finally, Aidan found his voice "What?" He didn't know what he had been expecting, but hearing the words spoken out loud made the idea more real.

"For you to be able to return home, you must kill Asmodeus," Gabrielle said.

"I heard you, but how can that be the only way. Can't he simply remove the barrier?" Aidan asked.

"He is extraordinarily stubborn, so he is unlikely to do so. Such barriers are fed from the energy of the creator, only once the soul has been destroyed can the barrier be removed." Gabrielle said.

"Are you sure that is the only way?" Aidan asked again, still reluctant to accept the conclusion.

"Of course, I am. Why do you wish to protect him so much? I did not realize you shared a friendship."

"He isn't my friend, but it doesn't mean that I want to kill him," Aidan answered, frowning at how Gabrielle could accept his death so easily. "Besides, what will happen to Azriel?"

At his mention of Azriel, Gabrielle looked away awkwardly. She was quiet for a time, giving Aidan a bad feeling before she spoke. "He – he is collateral damage, and an unfortunate loss. They share the same soul, and they cannot be separated."

Aidan clenched his jaw, hating the idea of killing Azriel. "Is there no other way?"

"None that I know of." She answered.

Aidan sat on the bed, and held his head in his hands as he considered his choices. He did not care for Asmodeus, but he still did not want to kill him. He could not stand the thought of hurting Azriel. He did not deserve to die so Aidan could go home.

"Asmodeus will not be expecting your attack, which makes the situation ideal," Gabrielle explained. "You can deliver a fatal blow during your sparring match when he expects only innocent strikes. If you strike quickly and accurately, you will have no fear of him realizing your intentions." She said reassuringly.

A vicious glint came into Gabrielle's eyes as she spoke of Asmodeus's death. Aidan did not notice however as he was lost in his thoughts. Zacharias sent a cautioning look in Gabrielle's direction, and she composed her expression into a gentler one.

Sensing his resistance, Gabrielle spoke again. "If you make it quick, Azriel does not need to suffer. He does not need to be aware of what is happening."

Aidan recalled what Azriel had told him of recalling certain things like a dream. He suspected that Azriel would witness the nightmare of Aidan delivering the fatal blow. Azriel would know that Aidan had betrayed him.

He looked back to his body. It was strange to think that he looked like he was sleeping when so much was happening. He desperately wished that this was some coma induced dream. Yet his experiences were too vivid. It was undeniably real.

Jazmine's image arose in his mind, and he felt the familiar ache of loneliness. Could he live with himself if he sacrificed Azriel to see her again? How would she feel if she knew what he had done? Maybe she could offer some insight. If she could forgive him, then maybe he could too.

"What do I have to do?" Aidan asked, resigning himself to the idea that he might have to kill Azriel, the very thought made him sick.

"Fatally injure Asmodeus during one of your sparring matches. Once you have done so, you can absorb both Asmodeus and Azriel's power. You cannot leave Azriel's power untouched. Doing so would allow Asmodeus to regain his strength, and return to take revenge. Do you understand?" Gabrielle said, watching him carefully.

"Yes," said Aidan numbly, still hating himself for even considering the idea. "What about after?"

"When the task is done, return to me, and we will tear apart the barrier together. With their power at your command, you will have all the strength you need to finally be able to go home." Gabrielle said. "Azriel's sacrifice will allow you to return home."

"You can't come with me to defeat Asmodeus?"

"No, he will become suspicious if I attend your training sessions. Besides, you are skilled enough to defeat him alone, as you have demonstrated." Gabrielle said proudly.

"What do I say if he asks what you wanted?"

"Say that I felt you weren't ready, and sent you back for further training. The ruse will encourage him to train you more, giving you the opportunity you need." Gabrielle came to sit beside him, and took his hand in hers. "Be cautious that Asmodeus does not suspect your plan before you are prepared. Act as if you know nothing, and we will not fail." She was quiet to allow him a moment before speaking again. "Should we return to Azriel's home?"

"I can find my own way back. I'd rather stay here for a little while." Aidan said, finally looking at Gabrielle.

"As you wish, Aidan." Gabrielle rested her hand on his shoulder. "Do not hesitate to seek me out if you need anything." She placed a gentle kiss on his forehead. "You will be home before you know it."

"Thanks, Gabrielle." He said.

With a final nod, Gabrielle and Zacharias vanished. Hanging his head, Aidan rested his elbows on his knees.

≈≈≈≈≈≈≈≈≈

Aidan appeared in Jazmine's room, startling the cat which lounged on Jazmine's lap while she studied. The cat hissed, and arched its back, digging his claws into her leg, before he leapt away, and ran from the room. Jazmine cringed as the cat left bloody claw marks on her legs.

"Damn it Pretzel! What's wrong with you?" She said angrily, and then turned around to watch as the cat bolted from the room. As she turned, she caught sight of the cause of the cat's panic. "Aidan!" She exclaimed, and then grinned. "I thought I had dreamt your visit."

He forced a smile, happy to see her, but unable to shake his dismal mood. "Hey, Jazz. Sorry I haven't come back sooner. I have been busy with training." His tone was subdued, feeling like a guilty child who had come to admit his wrongdoing.

Aidan looked at the scratches on her leg, and frowned. "I guess Pretzel doesn't know what to think of me like this. Come sit on the bed, I want to try something."

He moved to the bed, and sat. As Jazmine joined him he placed his hand over the scratches. As before, he could not make physical contact with her. Curious to see if healing would work, he concentrated on the image of her skin joining together. Jazmine shivered a bit, feeling cold where his hand hovered, but the coolness soothed the pain of the scratches. As he moved his hand away, her eyebrows raised in surprise.

"Wow, you have learned a lot," Jazmine said, running her fingers over the skin. Only faint scars remained.

Aidan shrugged. "I guess I've finally gotten the hang of being a ghost. But I still can't figure out how to finally be able to touch you." He added sadly. Aidan held his hand close to her cheek, remembering how soft her skin felt.

"I'll be glad to have you back." She whispered, moving her head so her cheek would have pressed against his hand if contact had been possible. "Were you at the hospital a few days ago Aidan?"

"No, why?" He asked curiously.

"I thought I caught a glimpse of you again," Jazmine said, frowning, and looking uncertain. "Maybe I imagined it. I wanted to see you."

Aidan frowned slightly, puzzled by what she said. "Stranger things have happened over the last couple of weeks. It wasn't me, but do you remember what he looked like?" Aidan asked. Maybe Asmodeus had returned to reinforce the barrier, and ensure he couldn't escape.

"I only caught a quick glimpse, but it looked like he was standing by the nurse. He was tall, and he had white hair, and a beard. I can't remember anything else about him." Jazz answered, trying to recall specific details of the man. Her memory of him was vague however, and she shook her head, frustrated. "Sorry, I didn't get a good look."

"It was probably nothing." Aidan said as he nodded, feeling somewhat disappointed that her description didn't match Asmodeus. Maybe it wasn't him, and Jazz had caught a glimpse of another Aduro or Shade.

"It seemed strange." Jazz said, thinking back to the visit. She recalled the nurse's strange behavior, and frowned. "Even the nurse was acting odd. It was like she felt something was different too. She was all jumpy, and left pretty quick after giving you some medication." Jazz was quiet for a moment. "I'm glad you came, I have wanted to talk to you."

"About what?" Aidan asked.

"While I was at the hospital, I spoke with the doctor. He said your vitals are weakening and things aren't looking as good. It seems like the stronger you get there, the weaker your body becomes here." She said quietly, finally admitting what she had been trying to avoid.

"I guess it's a good thing that I should be able to return home soon." He said quietly, his gaze wandering the room to avoid looking at her. The clock was ticking, so he would have to make his move quickly if he ever hoped to return to his body.

"Gabrielle has finally said you are ready?"

"She has," Aidan said, although his miserable tone did reflect what should have been good news.

"What's wrong, Aidan?" She asked, concerned. She felt her stomach twist, as she anticipated the news.

"I have to kill Asmodeus."

Jazmine hesitated for a moment, trying to understand exactly what was happening. "But he trained you."

"And he is also the one who is keeping me from returning to my body, because he wants me to replace him," Aidan explained, finally looking back at Jazmine, and watching her expression.

"So if he is keeping you there, then he isn't giving you much of a choice." Jazz reasoned. She didn't want to sound cold, but if Aidan was going to be able to return home, he would have to do what was needed. "Maybe you can reason with him?" She said, hoping for a better outcome.

"I doubt it," Aidan said grimly, knowing that Asmodeus was stubborn at the best of times. He did not see Asmodeus being convinced, and as Gabrielle had indicated, surprise was his ally in this fight. "But it also means that Azriel must die," Aidan whispered, finally arriving at the point that bothered him the most.

Understanding dawned on Jazmine as Aidan spoke. She remembered how fondly Aidan had spoken of Azriel, and frowned. "Oh." She said. "So what will you do?"

"I want to come home, so I guess I don't have much of a choice," Aidan said grimly. "I hate that Azriel has to be involved. He doesn't deserve to pay for Asmodeus's betrayal."

"I know he is like a Father to you." Jazz said, reaching for his hand, and then stopping herself. So much for being able to offer a comforting touch.

Aidan paused, considering her assessment of Azriel. He hadn't stopped to consider his relationship with Azriel, but now he realized that it was the relationship he wished he could have with his Father. It only made his coming actions even harder. Azriel was the closest thing to a proper Father he would likely ever have.

"I hadn't thought of him like that, but you are right." He said, looking away to hide his pained expression. "I have to betray him to return home. Hardly seems fair."

"Oh Aidan. This isn't fair at all." She said unhappily. "What can I do to help?"

"Be there when I wake up from this nightmare." He said, looking down at his hands miserably.

Nineteen...

"A single lie destroys a whole reputation of integrity."
- Baltasar Gracian

When Aidan returned, he found Asmodeus sitting at the oak desk in the study. He had positioned another armchair directly across from the desk. Asmodeus took slow sips of his drink, enjoying how the energy flowed through him. He spared a rare smile as Aidan entered the room as if amused by some private joke.

"You have returned. I assume Gabrielle has finished spinning her web of lies?" He asked cruelly.

"I don't know what you are talking about," Aidan replied, rather unnerved by Asmodeus's perception of the situation. Had he somehow listened in on their conversation? Could he have followed him? A series of paranoid thoughts ran through his mind, but they all seemed unlikely.

"Come now, Aidan. I know you don't care for me, but please don't insult my intelligence. It does not take a genius to know that Gabrielle would be thrilled to be rid of me, especially now that she has a new pet." He said, beginning to look smug as Aidan looked more uncomfortable.

"If she did want to get rid of you that is your own fault. You aren't exactly the most trustworthy of servants." Aidan responded sharply. Gabrielle didn't treat him like that.

Asmodeus laughed heartily, genuinely amused by Aidan's retort. "Gabrielle likes her pets to be obedient, as you will find out. But please enlighten me. What are the specific lies that she has been spreading now? I am sure they are entertaining."

Aidan hesitated for a moment, but it seemed that attempting to maintain secrecy was not an option. Clearly, Asmodeus would be on his guard. Entering into a sparring session with him now could prove to be a fatal mistake. Yet it seemed all too fitting for him to reveal that he knew Asmodeus's plan. At least that might wipe the smug expression off his face.

"Gabrielle told me your plan. You were at my house, and then at the hospital. Things started to make sense once she explained it."

"Yes, I believe we established that already since we both clearly remember those events. Unless you are experiencing some amnesia." Asmodeus said smoothly, still grinning smugly.

"But she told me what you were doing there," Aidan answered accusingly.

"And what devious plots have I concocted without my own knowledge?"

"You influenced my father, and triggered the fight that caused my coma. Now you are trying to keep me here until my body dies. Then I can replace you." Aidan said quickly, puzzled by Asmodeus's calm reaction. He had expected him to fly into a rage as his plot was revealed, but Asmodeus wasn't acting in a way that made sense. "She is getting crafty in her old age. And how did she come across this knowledge?" Asmodeus asked.

He was content to reverse roles , and ask countless questions like Aidan normally did.

"Zacharias saw you there, but couldn't stop you."

"So she has Zacharias wrapped around her finger as well. I suppose that should not surprise me. He always followed her like a lost mutt." Asmodeus said, speaking more to himself than Aidan. He seemed distracted for a moment as he pieced the situation together in his mind. Slowly her devious plot became clear to him, and he smirked slightly. Gabrielle had not gathered so much power by being dumb, that was for certain.

"I suppose you haven't even considered the idea that he influenced the fight. Consider for a moment that I observed from across the street, too far to have any influence over what occurred. In fact, it was that distance which prevented me from calming the situation." Asmodeus added in a bored tone.

"Why should I? You're probably trying to protect yourself by lying to me." Aidan demanded.

"As I thought," Asmodeus replied dryly, then dismissed the topic. "Tell me, when did she advise you to kill me?"

"I was supposed to kill you during a sparring match. But I think I prefer a fair fight." Aidan answered coldly.

This seemed to amuse Asmodeus. "Oh kid, you are funny. Do you think you can win against me in a fair fight?"

"I won last time."

"Did you?" Asmodeus asked, implying what Aidan already suspected.

Aidan thought back to their sparring match, recalling how Asmodeus had not been the same while Zacharias had watched. The fight hadn't been an easy win, but Asmodeus had made many mistakes which were out of character for him. Even at the time, it had even felt like a cheap victory.

"You are too arrogant to have let me win intentionally," Aidan responded, fishing for answers.

"My healthy sense of self-preservation outweighs my ego," Asmodeus said with a smirk. "I am not a fool; I can see how much Gabrielle hates me. It is not difficult to imagine that she would want me gone. Anticipating her intentions regarding your training, I let you win so she would be fooled into thinking you are ready."

"I could still win."

"Are you willing to gamble your life on that?" Asmodeus cautioned, the picture of confidence as he held Aidan's gaze.

Aidan considered Asmodeus's question carefully. He questioned his own skill, and found him doubting his chances of success. Unless Asmodeus was bluffing, but did he dare risk his life on suspicion of a bluff.

"It seems not," Asmodeus commented bleakly. "And frankly, I have no desire to risk my life either, even if the odds are in my favour. So how about we take a moment to consider our present situation, and the associated facts before we quite foolishly launch into combat?"

After weighing his options for a moment, Aidan sighed. "I'll hear what you have to say," Aidan said. Perhaps he could fool Asmodeus into thinking that he had sided with him, and then strike when he wasn't anticipating it. It was a deceitful tactic, but open combat was risky. Mentally he prepared to form his weapons quickly in case Asmodeus was luring him as well.

"Consider for a moment that you are relying solely on one source of information. A rather foolish position to be in, as I see it." Asmodeus said. As he spoke, he reached for the decanter on his desk, and poured Aidan a glass. He met Aidan's gaze as he slid the glass across the desk to him. "Sit, please." Asmodeus motioned to the armchair facing the desk.

Aidan took the glass reluctantly, but did not drink from it. He wondered for a moment if there was such a thing as poison in this realm. He took a seat across from Asmodeus, keeping as much distance between them as possible. He held the glass in his hands, trying to appear as relaxed as his opponent. Aidan recalled when he had played chess with Azriel in this same manner.

"So Gabrielle has suggested that I wish to keep you here as my replacement. Yet I can't help, but point out that I have been forced to babysit you for the duration of your time here. Why should I inflict such torment upon myself?"

"To be free from Gabrielle for the long term. I was supposed to replace you eventually, she said you wished to hurry that fate."

"She played the fate card, did she? Gabrielle likes to pretend that she knows the future. However, she uses the word fate to make her own desires seem more important. Her understanding of fate is that we are pawns to be moved according to her will."

"Or is that your understanding?"

"You are wrapped up in her spell, aren't you?" Asmodeus rolled his eyes. "Consider who else was at the house the night you bumped your head."

"Zacharias," Aidan admitted, knowing that Gabrielle had verified that fact. "But why would he try to influence the fight?"

"He would have been acting under Gabrielle's orders."

Aidan shook his head, beginning to feel angry that Asmodeus would try to bring Gabrielle's intentions into question. "You are trying to protect yourself. It's no secret that you don't like me, and have no desire to help me get home."

"If you don't believe me, at least consider the possibility for Azriel's sake," Asmodeus advised. "To kill me in combat could also mean killing him."

"I have considered that, which is the worst part of this whole thing. Azriel shouldn't have to pay for your lies." Aidan said.

Finally, Asmodeus seemed to lose all patience. "I've had enough of this. If you are too thick headed to listen to sense, get out of my presence." He growled, his change in mood making the room uncomfortably hot.

Just as furious, Aidan got up and turned to leave. He would deal with Asmodeus soon enough. He had to wait for his guard to be down.

Aidan strode towards the doorway, eager to be away from Asmodeus. As he reached the doorway, he found it blocked by an impassable wall. Instantly he recognized the barrier as the same kind which kept him from his body. He seethed at Asmodeus's arrogance. How dare he taunt him like this. As Asmodeus began to laugh at him, Aidan spun around with his blade forming in his hand.

"This proves it," Aidan said through clenched teeth.

"It proves nothing if you take a moment to recall Azriel's lessons about powerful influences. I believe he said a powerful influence, leaves a mark." Asmodeus said slyly, seeking to awaken Aidan's memory.

Aidan hesitated, knowing that there was truth to his words. He considered for a moment. Was this more deception, or was there truth to what Asmodeus said after all?

Feeling some reluctance, he reached out towards the barrier while keeping his eyes on Asmodeus. His hand met the invisible barrier, and he could feel its strength. Asmodeus's familiar rage kept him at bay, and lashed out at him as he made contact.

He could not deny that this barrier had no resemblance to the one that surrounded his body. As usual, Asmodeus's creations were harsh, and unyielding, but the wall around his body had kept him out with calm patience. No creation of Asmodeus's would act with such pastoral resilience; only Gabrielle was so unwaveringly tranquil.

It was strange that he should be betrayed by Gabrielle when it was Asmodeus who appeared to be the untrustworthy one. As he finally accepted the reality of Asmodeus's words, he let his sword vanish.

"Why would she do this?" Aidan asked, trying to decipher her motives as he adjusted to the reality of her deception.

"I suspect that she has been honest about her motives, despite her lying about them being my wishes," Asmodeus said. "She views me as a threat, especially as my power grows. Gabrielle fears that one day I will tire of her rule, and overthrow her. She is uncertain if I am truly stronger than her, so she will not risk an honest battle with me. Rather she wishes to use you because she considers you expendable. If you fail, then she thinks I will assume that the attack was your own doing."

"And aren't you tired of her?"

"I grew tired of her long ago, but I have never made plans to move against her," Asmodeus answered cynically. "She is convinced that I will. She refuses to believe that I accept the natural order of things. If I were to overthrow her, I would be overrun with annoying

Shades. Presently I enjoy their fear of me because I hunt them down when they misbehave."

It was exactly the type of answer he expected from Asmodeus. Of course, Asmodeus would take delight in his darker talents being employed. It was a natural calling for him to become a bounty hunter.

"So why would she try to have you killed now?"

"I imagine because I defied her order recently. She concluded she could not control me any longer if I chose to ignore her." He explained. "She also finally found someone whose anger rivals my own, and therefore would make a worthy opponent. You."

Aidan was surprised by Asmodeus's backhanded compliment. It might have been the first; although perhaps not a positive observation. "And what would she have done with me?"

"I believe she would have kept you here as my replacement. With me gone she would have needed someone to do her dirty work. Despite my criticisms, you are strong, but have a good heart so she would have trusted you." Asmodeus admitted begrudgingly.

Returning slowly to his chair, Aidan perched on the edge of it cautiously. He was still not at ease with Asmodeus, but couldn't deny his words. "What do we do then?"

"Once she realizes that we know of her plan, Gabrielle will try to have us both killed as we have become liabilities," Asmodeus predicted. "She will know that I feel obliged to kill her for her betrayal. Of course, you would no longer be a loyal subject if you were trapped here, and knew it was her doing, so naturally, you would have to go as well."

Aidan was unsettled by his answer. He would have to make a choice. Gabrielle might have been attempting to protect her rule by removing Asmodeus, but that did not change the nature of her deception. Yet to kill Gabrielle was to unleash Asmodeus with no one to harness his fury, a dangerous prospect.

"Can't she take down the wall?"

"She would not risk leaving me alive, especially once she knows I saw through her scheme. I suspect that she wishes to keep you here, and even now attempts to have your body perish." Asmodeus swirled his drink slowly in his glass. "Gabrielle would not risk leaving someone alive who is a threat to her. She made that mistake when she recruited me. However, I have a plan to test her honesty in relation to sending you home."

Aidan arched a brow, and waited for Asmodeus to continue. Finally picking up his own glass again, he took a sip. For the first time since his meeting with Gabrielle, he was beginning to feel hope that he would not have to betray Azriel.

Asmodeus also took a sip of his own drink before continuing. "We meet her deception, with a lie of our own. Trick her into thinking you have killed me. If she allows you to return home, then she will have redeemed herself. If not, then she will suffer for betraying you."

"And what of you?"

"I am content to disappear into the shadows if she lets you go. I am tired of being her assassin. If she believes I am dead, I have no reason to prove her otherwise." He answered.

"You don't want revenge on her for trying to have you killed?"

Asmodeus smiled at the question. "Anyone who has ever tried to kill me is dead. It will be amusing to allow her to believe she has finally succeeded." He laughed again, enjoying his own twisted humor about the situation.

"So how do we trick her?"

"That is the part which I imagine you will not like," Asmodeus said, and his expression sobered as he thought of his plan.

"Azriel must be sacrificed."

~~~~~~~~~

Yet again, Aidan was faced with the prospect of Azriel dying for him. With the revealing of Gabrielle's lies, he had hoped his mentors life could have been spared, but it seemed it wouldn't be so. He sat motionless for some time, trying to arrive at the same conclusion that Asmodeus had, and therefore a way around it.

"What do you mean?" Aidan asked finally, not entirely sure he wished to hear the explanation. "How can Azriel be sacrificed and you survive? Aren't you the same?"

Asmodeus looked smug. "Gabrielle has made the same assumption, but I have long suspected otherwise. Our powers are so different that they must come from separate sources. I have made many attempts to draw on his ability to heal, but I cannot. He is always the one to heal our injuries." He said, watching Aidan closely.

"So you think Azriel could be destroyed but you will survive?" Aidan said, following his train of thought.

"Precisely." Asmodeus said. "You must drain Azriel's power when he is in control." He explained.

"Are you sure it works like that?"

"Not entirely." Asmodeus admitted. "But it is a very educated guess."

Aidan frowned, considering the information carefully. He could only assume that if Gabrielle had known that this could be possible, she would have tried to destroy Asmodeus long ago. He could see why Asmodeus had never made the knowledge known.

"We may be able to fool Gabrielle into sending you home if she thinks the deed is done. However, she will need proof. If you can demonstrate that you have absorbed Azriel's power, she will believe that we are destroyed." Asmodeus explained. "She will not know the difference."

"Wouldn't it make more sense for me to absorb your power to show her that you are gone? You don't want to sacrifice yourself. You would rather have Azriel make the sacrifice. It's a win-win situation for you." Aidan said bitterly, suddenly realizing that Asmodeus wasn't so fearless. "You are a coward after all."

Asmodeus rolled his eyes, choosing to let the insult go. "No, I am practical. If Gabrielle does betray you, and attempts to keep you here, you will need my skills to dissuade her from doing so. Azriel could not fight

Gabrielle, which is why you must accept the fact that you need me."

Aidan sighed bitterly, seeing some logic in the argument. Azriel did not have the combat skills to force Gabrielle to let him go. His hope had to rest with Asmodeus, but it betraying Azriel... He loathed himself for even considering it.

"If I need you to defeat Gabrielle, why don't we fight her together?" Aidan challenged.

"You have forgotten about Zacharias. He would stand with her in battle, so the odds would be against us." Asmodeus reminded him. "The element of surprise is essential."

Aidan watched Asmodeus carefully, for the first time he noticed that his confidence had wavered. "You don't know if you can defeat her." He observed, sounding surprised.

"I am not one to gamble unnecessarily," Asmodeus said dryly.

"You will sacrifice Azriel, so you don't have to risk yourself. I thought you said I should listen to you to spare Azriel." Aidan said.

"I said that to get you to listen, and see reason. Unfortunately, his sacrifice is necessary." Asmodeus said, and pulled a cigar from his pocket. As he lit it, he watched Aidan. "If it reassures you at all, Azriel would make the sacrifice willingly for you. He is quite fond of you for some strange reason." As he spoke, smoke curled from his lips, and drifted away.

"I can't ask him to do that," Aidan said. "It's not right."

"I don't think you would have to ask. He would do it willingly if I know anything about Azriel. Besides, you are protecting him by sparing him the pain of Gabrielle's betrayal. He practically worships her." Asmodeus took another drag of his cigar. "But if you are squeamish about him knowing, don't tell him, and make it quick. That way you don't have to look into his eyes. I will conceal our plan from him so you do not have to fear him finding out."

"God, you are heartless," Aidan lamented.

"No, as I mentioned before, I'm practical," Asmodeus answered, breathing out smoke, and watching it swirl away. "If you want to go home, it's a trait you should learn."

"I'm not like you."

"But you are. That's why Gabrielle picked you. Your anger rivals my own. So as much as you pretend you aren't like me, you are." He answered.

"Well, I will never act like you."

"Another attribute which Gabrielle selected you for and it is why you ended up in this situation initially. You have all the power, but lack the questionable ethics to threaten her reign." Asmodeus said with a chuckle. "It is ironic really."

Aidan brooded silently for a time, not wanting to engage in the line of conversation with Asmodeus. "When would I have to do this?"

"Ideally, as soon as possible. We need to return you home before your body perishes." Asmodeus advised. "So when you have the opportunity, take it."

Aidan didn't acknowledge Asmodeus's words. Instead, he stood. Silently he left the room, unwilling to look at Azriel's malicious counterpart. The thought of what he had to do rested heavily on his shoulders. Hopefully, time would reveal some alternative, although time wasn't on his side.

Twenty...

"Truth is the daughter of time,
and I feel no shame in being her midwife."
- Johannes Kepler

Aidan spent the next two days avoiding Azriel. He was aware that delaying threatened his ability to return home, but he could not bring himself to face his mentor. Instead, he stayed away from the cottage entirely.

For a while longer, he wanted to be in denial about his present situation. He pretended that he didn't have to betray the one person who had aided him selflessly. Gabrielle and Asmodeus had both used him to further their own means, and would not hesitate to do so again. Azriel, on the other hand, had only tried to ensure his well-being.

Since learning about Gabrielle's betrayal, and Asmodeus's plan, Aidan had tried unsuccessfully to think of a way to save Azriel. Despite many flawed ideas, he could think of nothing besides simply staying. Yet Asmodeus had said that even that would fail once Gabrielle realized that Asmodeus was alive. It seemed that he was trapped in a situation he could not win.

To avoid Azriel, he spent his time divided between visiting Jazmine, and checking on his Mother. He spent long hours talking to his Mother, although she never heard a word he said. He consoled himself with the knowledge that his presence could provide her with some comfort. In fact, she seemed to improve a bit each time he visited, despite the lingering sadness, which he knew he could not remove entirely.

Aidan also took some time to visit his Father. He remained passive when he visited, no longer feeling the same need for revenge. He used the time to reflect on everything that had happened. He compared his relationship with his Father, to his relationship with Azriel. It was when he was with his Father that he felt the greatest change within himself. Yet this newfound strength did not help him deal with what he had to do. That was something he could not escape, no matter how much he had changed. It was the knowledge that he could not avoid Azriel much longer, which finally forced him to return to the cottage.

Aidan paused at the gate, staring past the fence. Walking into the garden no longer felt like a homecoming. Taking a deep breath, he passed through the gate, and into the garden. His anxiety was eased as he felt Azriel's soothing influence wash over him. He resisted the calm emotions, not wanting the guilt to be washed away so easily.

Masking his discomfort, Aidan searched for Azriel. Drawn to his calming presence, he found him standing in a sunny part of the garden watching a robin tend to her chicks. His expression was relaxed and content. Aidan approached silently, certain that Azriel had not noticed him yet.

"It is amazing, isn't it?" Azriel said, surprising Aidan.

"What is?" Aidan asked, watching the birds, and wondering what exactly Azriel was thinking. He stood beside his mentor with his hands thrust into his pockets. It was comforting to hear his Azriel's observations like nothing had changed.

"The lengths which robins will go to care for their young. The mother will land in front of a predator, and fake an injury to lure the threat away from her young. She places herself in harm's way to give her offspring a better chance at survival." Azriel said, watching the birds affectionately.

"I didn't know that," Aidan said, wondering why Azriel had decided to tell him this.

"The protective instinct of a parent is profound." He said, and then lapsed back into silence.

Aidan stole a glance at Azriel, and then looked back to the birds. The robin glided back to its nest, and tucked a worm into the chick's open mouths. Only to fly away again, in search of more food. The chicks quieted between the mother's visits, but clamored for attention upon her return. Despite their demanding ways, the mother robin tended to them with endless patience.

Aidan turned away from the nest, and retreated a few steps, suddenly uncomfortable. Azriel's comments served to evoke his guilt further. It seemed like he knew what was going to happen, and was reassuring Aidan. But he couldn't know. Asmodeus had promised to keep their plan secret. Unless Asmodeus had decided to taunt Azriel cruelly.

Aidan hesitated for a moment, trying to gather the determination to complete his task. Steeling his resolve was difficult however as he imagined Azriel's betrayed expression. A faint light started to glimmer to life in his hand as the sword began to form. He kept his eyes on Azriel's back, trying to reawaken the fury, which had filled him when he had first arrived in this netherworld. Maybe if he gave into that blind anger, he could complete the deed.

"You are no longer avoiding me?" Azriel asked, finally breaking the silence, and turning away from the birds. As Azriel turned, the light in Aidan's hand vanished, and he forced a strained smile.

"I haven't been avoiding you," Said Aidan.

"I didn't think our relationship was based on lies, Aidan." He said calmly, his expression and voice as kind as ever.

Aidan quickly looked away, unable to hold his gaze. He searched for something to engage his attention.

"You have not spoken to me since your meeting with Gabrielle. I assume that she deemed you ready since your training with Asmodeus has ceased. Yet you are still here, so your task is still incomplete."

Aidan nodded stiffly, and then was motionless as he struggled to control his body language. Azriel could read him so easily that anything might give his discomfort away. Yet even as he tried to mask any tell, he only appeared more awkward. He dreaded the moment when Azriel would question him.

"So, when will you complete the task you were assigned?"

"I'm not sure exactly." He said slowly, trying to sound casual. "But it will have to be soon. Jazz said my body is weakening. So if I want to be able to go home, I have to act." He added.

Azriel nodded thoughtfully, as he considered the information. "I am surprised that your body is weakening so quickly. You are young, strong, and eager to return to your body. These things should have strengthened your connection."

Aidan frowned now as he considered Azriel's words. He thought back to what Jazmine had told him earlier, and he began to suspect foul play. "Jazz said that she saw someone at the hospital when the nurse was there, and that the nurse was acting strangely. Could someone be influencing the nurse to make me worse?" he said to Azriel.

It didn't take any stretch of the imagination to conclude who would want to weaken his body. Initially, he had suspected Asmodeus, but now the pieces were falling into place. Jazz had said the man had been tall with grey hair. The description fit Zacharias all too well, only confirming what Asmodeus had already convinced him of.

"It would take a powerful influence to persuade the nurse to go against her natural caring instinct, but it could be possible with enough time, and the right approach," Azriel said, deeply troubled by the news. "It will only be a matter of time before your body is poisoned beyond repair if this is the case."

Aidan took a deep breath, trying to calm his rising anger. Azriel glanced at him, sensing the shift in his mood, but said nothing.

It seemed that Gabrielle was capable of all kinds of treachery. She had even gone so far as to conspire to keep him here. How long had Zacharias been influencing the nurse to poison him under Gabrielle's orders?

"We need to stop him then before I get any worse." Aidan said, managing to catch himself before he said Zacharias's name. Azriel did not need to know about Gabrielle's involvement. Asmodeus was right that Azriel shouldn't have to suffer the betrayal of a trusted ally.

"You speak as if you know who it is."

"Of course not," Aidan said unconvincingly.

Azriel didn't question him for information. Instead, he addressed the most pressing matter of what they were going to do. "First, we must find a way to protect your body from further harm, then we can form the next stage of our plan."

Aidan thought for a moment, and then answered. "Jazz could stay at the hospital, and make sure I am not given anything else." Aidan suggested.

"Good, even if she is being influenced, it is highly doubtful that she would risk getting caught, especially if she is compelled by an influence." Azriel said.

Aidan nodded in agreement. "I'll tell her." He said, and prepared to leave. Hopefully, this could buy him more time to plan a way to save Azriel.

"Wait." Azriel cautioned. "We need to prepare. Gabrielle may accelerate her plans by having the nurse deliver a fatal dose sooner. We need to be prepared."

For a moment he didn't think anything of it as Azriel spoke Gabrielle's name. It seemed only natural to be discussing this with Azriel. He tried to recall if he had said anything which might have revealed her betrayal.

"What do you mean?" Aidan said, trying to sound casual.

"It is kind of you to wish to protect me, but it is not I who needs protecting. You are the one who is risking everything by delaying your task." Azriel said gently, reminding him of the limited time.

"You know?" Aidan said, his voice hushed.

"It is no secret that she hates Asmodeus. I thought she would have challenged him before this, but he has grown so powerful that she doubts her skills. It doesn't surprise me that she would find another, so she does not have to risk herself. I was suspicious of her motives as soon as she assigned Asmodeus to watch over you." He said, slowly walking through the garden as he spoke. "Her insistence that he train you only confirmed my suspicions. She seemed too eager to limit the contact I had with you. I imagine she wanted you to hate Asmodeus, and have no contact with me so you would not struggle with the decision to kill us."

"Is that why you insisted on training me as well?" Aidan fell in step alongside Azriel, soothed by their usual routine of walking in the garden.

"Not at all. I knew there were certain lessons that Asmodeus would not be able to teach you. You could not expect to function in this realm without knowing how to protect yourself from influences."

Aidan thought back to his first lesson with Azriel, and understood the wisdom now. Then he recalled Azriel's warning as he prepared to meet Gabrielle for the first time. "That is why you taught me how to shield myself before you took me to see Gabrielle."

Azriel nodded. "Yes, I wanted you to be able to protect yourself from her charming ways. Otherwise, her influence might have overwhelmed you."

"You knew this whole time?"

"I had hoped I was wrong, but unfortunately I wasn't." He said sadly. "Gabrielle has become far too comfortable with using others as pawns."

Aidan nodded, once again surprised by Azriel's perception. It seemed that there was little that he missed. He was somewhat relieved that Azriel was already aware of Gabrielle's questionable actions. Yet that did not unburden him regarding the plan that Asmodeus had suggested. That still weighed heavily on him.

"You and Asmodeus both thought you could spare me from Gabrielle's deception. However, Asmodeus has yet to acknowledge that I am not naive. I may choose to not manipulate others, but that does not mean I cannot see the behavior occurring."

"So why haven't you said anything if you knew about this?" Aidan asked, puzzled by Azriel's lack of interference.

"I had no desire to manipulate you as Gabrielle and Asmodeus have done. I felt that it was best that you have a chance to form your own opinion. I imagine Asmodeus's plan is the reason why you have been avoiding me for the past few days." He said, watching Aidan carefully now.

"Why would I avoid you because of the plan?"

"It is a plan that you dislike, but an efficient one nonetheless." He said, meeting Aidan's gaze with unwavering calm.

Aidan looked away quickly, realizing that once again he couldn't hide anything from Azriel. "Asmodeus was to conceal the plan." He asked angrily, swearing to himself that Asmodeus would pay for his treachery.

"He did, but it shouldn't surprise you that we reached the same conclusion for different reasons," Azriel said in a low tone, subtly calming Aidan. "If Asmodeus had not suggested it, I would have."

"You don't even know what he suggested."

Azriel didn't bother with a response as he waited for Aidan to accept what they both knew. Instead, he focused on enjoying the garden, including the warm sunshine, and singing birds. Despite the knowledge that it would all end soon, he was content.

"Why?" Aidan finally asked in a strained voice.

"I'm afraid I don't understand the question," Azriel responded kindly.

"Why would you sacrifice yourself? That is the same conclusion we've all reached, isn't it?"

"It is," Azriel confirmed calmly.

"Then why? I'm not special. I don't deserve that sacrifice."

"To start, you think you don't deserve it, which usually suggests that you do. You give yourself too little credit." Azriel said. "Besides, you are young, and have yet to live your life. I have lived a human life, plus a long time in this realm. It is far more acceptable for my time to end."

"You are seriously pulling the 'I've lived too long' line?" Aidan asked. "Who actually wants to die?"

"Is it truly dying?" Azriel questioned. "Death in the human world brought us to this realm. Perhaps I will experience what is beyond this life."

Unconvinced, Aidan frowned. "You really want to die? What if there is nothing beyond this?" He pointed out, not wanting to accept Azriel's attempt to comfort him so easily.

"No one wants to die," Azriel answered. "But sometimes it is worth dying for a cause you believe in."

"So you would die for me?" Aidan said, still in disbelief.

"If Asmodeus won't, I will. I am prepared to do this. You want to go home, and this is how we can make it so. You clearly love Jazmine and, deserve to have a life with her." He said gently, trying to ease Aidan's doubts.

Aidan thought of Jazmine, and for the first time in a while, a slight smile touched his lips. This experience at least had made him realize how much he loved her.

"Here is what we will do." Azriel continued when Aidan did not respond. "You will go to Jazmine. Ask her to watch over your body. Explain what we suspect and that she must watch the staff carefully. Then you will return, and absorb my power. With my power, you can return to Gabrielle, and present evidence that your task is complete. If she doesn't allow you to return home, Asmodeus will deal with her. You will have to keep Zacharias from interfering. Are you prepared to duel with him?"

"I should be able to handle him." Aidan responded, "How tough can an old man be?" He joked, trying to make light of the situation.

Azriel did not seem to find it humorous. "Don't be fooled; he is a threat that shouldn't be taken lightly."

"If you say so," Aidan said, his humor only masking his anxiety.

"Once Gabrielle surrenders or is defeated, you will be able to return home by passing your energy back to your body," Azriel said. "It will be difficult, but I think you and Asmodeus stand the best chance of success."

"I wish it didn't have to be like this." Aidan lamented.

"It is best this way. Gabrielle must be given the opportunity to release you, or be taken by surprise if she doesn't." He said, sounding confident.

"Aren't you worried about what Asmodeus will do without you to keep him under control?" Aidan asked after a few moments of silence.

Azriel's expression became more serious as he considered Aidan's question. "I had considered it, but the risk is worth it. Gabrielle has proven to be manipulative and dangerous. If she is willing to interfere in the human realm and cause you harm to keep you here, there is no telling what else she will do. Asmodeus is a known quantity at least. He enjoys hunting Shades, and isn't manipulative."

"You don't think he's evil?"

Azriel chuckled. "If there is one thing I know about Asmodeus, it is that he is more complex than he seems. He is a dark being, but not outright cruel." Azriel said, considering his assessment carefully. "I suppose I could be taking a risk by trusting that he has morals, but I think that risk is worthwhile."

Aidan wasn't entirely reassured, but trusted Azriel's instincts. "So I guess I should go find Jazz, and tell her the plan."

"Yes that would be best. Return to me when she is prepared, and we will complete this once and for all."

≈≈≈≈≈≈≈≈

Jazz sat in the library, trying to focus on the textbook in front of her. She sighed, rubbing her forehead as she tried to make sense of what she was reading. As the end of the semester approached, school was proving to be more stressful than ever. Her teachers tried to be understanding and give her extra time, but there was only so much that they could do.

It didn't help that the whole school was aware of Aidan's coma, and she was constantly being asked how he was doing. The concern everyone showed was wonderful, but it only reminded her of the situation, and made it harder to focus. Desperate to escape some of the attention, she had fled to the library for her free period to finish her late biology assignment.

Rising from her chair, Jazz returned to the bookshelves to search for another reference book. Finding the section, she picked out three books which seemed to be promising for reference material. Jazz focused on the books, glancing over the table of contents to be sure it would be useful. She turned around to go back to her table, and found herself face to face with Aidan. Jazz yelped in surprise, and dropped her books. They landed on the floor with a loud bang, and the librarian peered around the shelf to shoot her a disapproving glare.

"Is something wrong?" The librarian asked.

"Sorry, thought I saw a spider." She said quickly in a quiet voice, and crouched down to gather up the books. When the librarian turned back to what she had been doing, Jazz spoke in a hushed tone to Aidan. "Geez, do you have to sneak up on me every time?"

"Sorry, I didn't mean to." Aidan apologized. "I need to talk to you."

"Over here." She whispered.

Going to the table, Jazz set down her books. She returned to the aisle, and searched for an isolated corner where she could talk with Aidan. Trying to look casual, she ignored him until they were out of sight of the other students, and the librarian. Glancing around a final time, she turned to him.

"Are you okay? Did you...?" She said, sounding worried. Jazz searched Aidan's expression, trying to judge how he was doing.

"Not yet. It turns out that Azriel knew all along. He is going along with Asmodeus's plan, though." Aidan explained hurriedly.

"He is going to sacrifice himself for you?" Jazz asked, and looked surprised when Aidan nodded. "Wow. He does care about you." She said, having a new respect for Azriel.

"I know," Aidan answered quietly. He was distracted for a moment as he thought of Azriel. He shook his head slightly, remembering why he was here. "But I need your help."

"I'll do anything I can."

"Do you remember the nurse you told me about?" Aidan asked and when Jazz nodded, he continued. "Azriel thinks that she is being influenced to poison me. Gabrielle wants to trap me here by killing my body. I need you to go to the hospital, and make sure that the nurse doesn't give me anything else."

"Like an Angel of Death? Are you sure it's her?" Jazz asked, thinking of the TV documentary she had seen about nurses who killed their patients.

"I don't know if it is her, but something isn't right. I'm hoping that whomever it is won't do anything if you are watching. Can you do that?"

"Of course! I'll go after school and stay."

Aidan shook his head. "No, I need you to go now if you can. Gabrielle might try to influence the nurse to finish it. We're lucky she hasn't so far."

"I'll tell the school I'm going home sick."

"Thanks, Jazz. Hopefully, this will all be over soon." He said.

"I hope so too." She answered.

"Jazz, in case things don't work out I want you to know something..." He started to say, but stopped when Jazz held up her hand.

"You can tell me when you wake up." She said confidently. "I can't wait to have you home."

Aidan smiled warmly. "Okay." He answered, knowing it would give him even more determination to fight.

"See you soon." She said as he vanished. "I love you too, Aidan." She whispered after he was gone.

Twenty-One...

*"Great achievement is usually born of great sacrifice,
and never the result of selfishness."*
– Friedrich Nietzsche

Aidan returned to the garden, and found Azriel waiting for him. He watched his mentor silently, at a loss for words. He had no idea how to say goodbye to someone who was making such a sacrifice. Sensing Aidan's presence, Azriel turned to face him, and rest his hand on his shoulder as reassurance.

"This is what is right."

"It doesn't feel right," Aidan said. "I don't know how I can live with myself knowing what I've done."

"The pain you are feeling won't last forever. Know that this is my choice."

"It doesn't feel like you had a choice at all." Aidan pointed out, feeling that Azriel had been cornered into the decision.

"I would have done this, even if Asmodeus had not suggested it," Azriel said. As he spoke, he began to pass his energy to Aidan. "Go live your life, and find happiness."

Aidan tried to resist receiving Azriel's power, but couldn't stop him from offering it to him. He finally accepted passively, having no desire to be a part of Azriel's demise. Still he could not help but be amazed by this energy that flowed into him, and was exhilarated by the sensation.

He felt like he had limitless reserves. The prospect of fighting Gabrielle and Zacharias did not seem as impossible now. He wondered how Azriel had ever feared them. Gradually, however, he felt the flow of power slow, and his elation was replaced by guilt.

Aidan looked into Azriel's eyes, and noticed the life leaving them. Azriel gave one last smile before his expression faded into nothing. Aidan felt the last of Azriel's power pass to him, and his throat constricted. Aidan struggled to control his emotions as Asmodeus manifested, and brought life back to the blank features.

Asmodeus looked him over coldly, no warmth in his expression. He removed his hand from Aidan's shoulder.

"Wow kid, I didn't think you had it in you," Asmodeus commented roughly.

"Shut up," Aidan said harshly, his voice both sad and angry. "Don't make stupid jokes about this."

"My apologies," Asmodeus said in a subdued tone which suggested that his apology was perhaps somewhat sincere. "Shall we finish this?"

Aidan nodded, and experimented with his newly received power. The power had Azriel's familiar presence to it, and he felt another stab of sorrow. He tried to ignore the feeling, focusing on the task as Azriel would have wanted him to. He would not waste Azriel's sacrifice. "Let's go." He said finally.

"Sounds good," Asmodeus said, and grinned cruelly, a malicious glimmer coming into his eyes. "Bring Gabrielle and Zacharias here, and I'll make a barrier so they cannot escape."

~~~~~~~~~

Aidan opened his eyes, and stared up at the outside of the cathedral. He could imagine Gabrielle relaxing in the bell tower, pleased with how her plans were coming together. He questioned how he had ever trusted her so blindly. Her deception made him furious, but he pushed the emotion away. He had to follow the plan, which meant not revealing what he knew. He composed himself, carefully sealing his emotions away and leaving only what he wished her to sense.

Aidan walked into the church, and looked around. The church was empty and silent. He paused for a moment, wondering what would happen when Gabrielle's presence was gone. Perhaps another Aduro would take up residence in the bell tower.

"Welcome back Aidan."

He turned as he heard Gabrielle's voice. She stood at the end of the aisle. Gabrielle gave him her typical radiant smile, and Aidan resisted the urge to scowl. He glanced around in search of Zacharias, wondering where his potential opponent was.

"Hi." He responded, trying to keep his tone civil.

"I was worried about you," Gabrielle said as she came forward, and embraced him. "I began to worry that Asmodeus had caught onto our plan."

"No, it went as we planned," Aidan answered, returning the embrace.

"So it is done?"

"Yes," Aidan replied. He released Gabrielle, and retreated a few steps. "Where is Zacharias? I thought he would have been with you." He felt a growing sense of concern. It was unusual for the disciple to not be nearby.

"I sent him to watch over your body while you dealt with Asmodeus. We will join him shortly." She said reassuringly, and then spoke again eagerly. "Show me your new power." She could not hide the eagerness she felt.

Her words did nothing to reassure him, only increase his sense of urgency. If Zacharias was influencing the nurse, he really was running out of time.

Aidan formed a sword in his hand, and it glowed brilliantly with Azriel's power.

Aidan shielded his mind from Gabrielle, not wanting her to sense his desire to strike at her while she was unprepared. He kept control however, knowing that it would be difficult to win in Gabrielle's domain.

Gabrielle nodded appreciatively. "Excellent." She said, a hint of envy in her voice.

Aidan allowed the sword to vanish as soon as he had her approval. He noticed the jealousy in her voice, realizing that she desired to have the power for herself. He would have to guard it carefully. "I'd like to go home now." He said, reminding her of the promise she had made.

"Of course!" She exclaimed. "How foolish of me. We will go at once." Gabrielle said, her warm smile returning.

~~~~~~~~

Jazz fidgeted impatiently as the elevator climbed to Aidan's floor. She shifted the textbooks uncomfortably in her arms. Stepping out of the elevator, She walked towards Aidan's room.

She gave a nod in greeting as she passed the nurse's desk, and they waved to her. If what Aidan suspected was true, then it was hard to feel overly friendly towards the nurses. But then again, the nurse whom she suspected was not at the station. Her stomach clenched nervously, as she walked faster.

Rounding the corner, she entered Aidan's room. Her heart skipped a beat as she arrived in time to see the nurse withdrawing a needle from Aidan's IV. Standing beside her, the transparent man Jazz had seen before stood whispering in her ear. Sensing that he was being watched, he looked up. Jazz made eye contact with him, and his eyes widened in surprise before he vanished suddenly.

"What are you doing?" Jazz demanded, setting her books down in the chair.

The nurse spun around, clearly not expecting anyone to have been watching. "Oh, you surprised me." She said unconvincingly. "I was giving him his medication." The nurse explained calmly, once she had regained her composure.

"The doctor never mentioned anything about medication to Sarah or me." Jazz answered just as calmly. She glanced at Aidan's body, but did not see any change for better or worse. Maybe the nurse had been telling the truth.

The nurse started to appear uncomfortable. "I'm sure he forgot to mention it."

"I'll go speak to him. I want to check on Aidan's progress anyway." Jazz responded. "Why don't you come with me?" she suggested as she slyly stole the empty bottle from the nurses cart without being noticed.

"I have my other patients to check on. If he has any questions, I will be doing my rounds." The nurse said, and retreated from the room quickly.

Jazz watched her go, slowly setting her bag down. Going to Aidan's bedside she gently kissed his cheek. "I hope I'm not too late." She whispered.

Going to the nurse's station, she smiled as she recognized one of the nurses she trusted. "Hey Jenn, is Dr. Briggs around? I need to talk to him." She said, trying to ignore the nervous fluttering in her stomach.

"I think he went on break, Jazz. Is there something I can do to help you?"

"Maybe..." Jazz hesitated for a moment, feeling strange bringing this up to another nurse. "There was a nurse in Aidan's room. She gave him a shot of something, but Dr. Briggs didn't say anything about medication to me?" Jazz asked, handing her the bottle.

Jenn frowned slightly and pulled up his chart on her computer. "I don't recall any meds being ordered. I'll page Doctor Briggs, and see if he prescribed something." The nurse looked troubled as she picked up the phone.

She had not even started to dial when alarms sounded on her computer. The nurse looked at the screen, and frowned. Pressing a button on an intercom, she spoke into it, and her voice carried over the speaker system. "Code blue, room 310."

Jazz's eyes widened as they paged Aidan's room number. She turned, and saw some nurses and doctors rushing to Aidan's room. She followed urgently, and heard Jenn trying to call her back. Jazz stopped in the doorway as one of the nurses blocked her way. "You have to wait here. I'm sorry, I can't let you in."

The heart monitor continued to show a flat line, and Jazz watched helplessly. "Aidan!" She yelled his name as a nurse restrained her.

~~~~~~~~~

Aidan and Gabrielle materialized in his hospital room. His stomach sank as he took in the chaotic scene of doctors. It was too late. He should have known that Zacharias would come here to finish what he had started. The solid drone of the heart monitor blared steadily in the background.

"I'm sorry Aidan, we are too late," Gabrielle said gently behind him.

Aidan looked towards the doorway as he heard Jazmine yell his name. The desperation in her voice sent a stab of pain through him. She was so upset that she didn't even notice him standing there. He would not give up. Aidan thought back to Azriel's healing lesson, and laughed internally. Azriel had given him all the skills he needed to return home.

"No, it isn't too late." He responded calmly.

Moving to the bedside, Aidan placed his hand on his body. The barrier still blocked him from returning, but that didn't matter. He closed his eyes, and called upon Azriel's power. He felt the energy rise, and flow through him willingly. As the doctors worked tirelessly to revive him, he fed his body the energy it needed to recover from the toxins effects.

Finally, the flat line of the heart monitor jumped to life, and gave an encouraging beep. Aidan grinned, and looked at Jazmine. He saw her knees weaken in relief, and her tears turn to a smile. He would keep fighting for her.

Behind him, he sensed Gabrielle's growing rage, and he turned to face her. "Good thing we arrived when we did." He said, watching her struggle to maintain her composure. "Now, release me so I can go home."

"What are you talking about?" Gabrielle said, looking concerned, but still attempting to charm him.

"Don't play dumb," Aidan said irritably. "You are behind all of this."

Gabrielle watched him for a moment, as she seemed to assess her options. Then her charming smile melted away into a sneer. "I saved you from a miserable mortal life."

"No, you took me away from the people I love, for your own gain." He answered harshly, relieved that he was finally able to challenge her openly.

"I don't understand you, Aidan. You are so eager to give up all this, for a mortal life. That mortal life will end one day, and you will be here eventually. Why not stay, and enjoy this power?" She said, trying to reason with him.

"I don't want this." He said passionately.

"Why? Do you not understand how much power you have now? You would never have to feel weak again if you stayed here."

"I never wanted to be here," Aidan answered. "It is not my time."

Gabrielle shook her head in frustration. "What a waste. You don't deserve his power."

"No amount of power is worth sacrificing a friend," Aidan replied coldly. "If you only valued Azriel for his power, then you didn't deserve to have him as a friend."

"I did value Azriel, but Asmodeus was too much of a threat to be allowed to live." Gabrielle insisted.

"You mean that he was too much of a threat to you. You were afraid that he would get tired of being bossed around." Aidan retorted, satisfied by her grim expression. "But I did what you wanted; they are gone. Now release me so that I can go home."

Gabrielle was silent for a long time, watching him greedily. "If you return, all of Azriel's power will be lost." She said, unable to hide the envy in her voice.

"If you want the power so badly, then take it. I want to go home." Aidan said, extending his hand out to her. He kept his expression passive, hiding his anger.

Gabrielle didn't deserve Azriel's power, and he could not risk giving it to her. If she became too powerful, Asmodeus might not be able to defeat her.

She watched him carefully, assessing cautiously. The temptation of power proved too great, and she slowly reached for his hand, grasping it tightly, paralyzing him with the force of her own will. Selfishly she tried to drain the power from him.

"With Azriel, Asmodeus, and your power, I will be even stronger. Don't fight, Aidan. It will be over soon." She said in a calm voice, trying to soothe him into giving up. She glanced behind him as Zacharias appeared to aide her.

As Aidan began to struggle, Zacharias restrained him by pulling his arms behind him. Gabrielle moved her hand to hold onto his shoulder roughly. He quickly built a mental defense to slow the draining of his power, but that only served to fuel her determination.

Aidan closed his eyes tightly, and thought of Azriel's garden. He felt the familiar tug, and then heard the birds singing in the trees. Surprised by the transportation, Zacharias loosened his grip, and Aidan broke free of the hold. He jumped away from them, and backed up to stand beside Asmodeus.

"Asmodeus?" Gabrielle hissed, her confusion quickly replaced by fury. "You are supposed to be dead." Aidan was pleased to see that for the first time, Gabrielle actually sounded afraid.

"By mortal standards, we are all dead. Well except for Aidan, he's comatose." Asmodeus responded practically, sounding like he was in good humor. His expression was particularly pleased as he enjoyed Gabrielle's reaction.

"You betrayed me!" Gabrielle hissed, turning her wrath towards Aidan.

Aidan laughed at the hypocrisy of her statement. "And I was foolish enough to trust you. What goes around, comes around." He answered in an amused voice, causing Asmodeus to shoot him a pleased smirk.

Gabrielle glanced around as if searching for some way out. Her expression became desperate as she sensed the barrier surrounding the garden.

"Don't worry; you aren't going anywhere." Asmodeus purred, practically gloating now. "You know, I was quite content to leave you alone. However, now you've forced me into action."

Gabrielle began to back up, putting more distance between herself and Asmodeus. He kept pace with her, however, not granting her the space. As Zacharias moved to stop him, Aidan stepped forward.

"Stay out of this," Aidan advised. "You were following her orders; and we can leave it at that if you don't interfere."

"You have no idea how long I have been waiting to dispose of Asmodeus," Zacharias answered with a cruel grin. "I have had to put up with his ego for far too long." He gloated as he formed two blades. Zacharias held the hilts of each weapon in his fist, and the single-edged blade curved over his knuckles, and finished into a deadly point.

"What about Azriel?" Aidan asked as he formed his sword and shield, crafting them with positive emotions as Azriel had taught him. They circled around each other, and searching for the other's weakness. Behind him, he was dimly aware that Gabrielle and Asmodeus were already locked in fierce combat.

"I do feel bad about Azriel," Zacharias answered, sounding sincere.

Aidan did not reply, watching his opponent carefully. Asmodeus had warned him not to be fooled by Zacharias's elderly appearance. Now that he watched him, Aidan saw how nimbly he moved, and the strength in his limbs.

"It must have been terrible to see his end," Zacharias said, intentionally toying with his emotions.

Aidan hesitated as he recalled Azriel's final moments. The memory was still fresh, and awoke painful memories.

In his moment of distraction, Zacharias attacked. Aidan quickly brought his shield up, blocking the sweeping blow. He felt the shield and blade clash, testing the strength of each other. As soon as the weapons met, he knew he was facing a strong opponent.

Aidan disengaged, retreating a few quick steps to give himself room. Zacharias did not give him any ground however as he continued to attack. Aidan was forced into a defensive position, blocking each blow, but never finding an opportunity to counter with one of his own. He hoped Zacharias would tire himself with the onslaught of attacks.

Nearby Gabrielle and Asmodeus swept around the garden in a frenzy of movement. They continuously exchanged blows, well matched in skill. What Gabrielle lacked in strength, she made up for in speed. Her dual swords forced Asmodeus to block, and dodge in fast sequence. His years of combat training served him well, as he countered each of her attacks. However, he seemed to lack his usual flourish, his movements slower than normal. He bided his time, waiting for Gabrielle to make a mistake.

Meanwhile, Aidan continued to struggle to gain the upper hand with Zacharias. They no longer circled each other. Instead they exchanged blows, and parrying stabs with deadly speed. They moved around the garden as they sidestepped each other's attacks. Zacharias feigned a blow, which Aidan moved to block, but as he did so, Zacharias slashed a deep wound into Aidan's arm with his other weapon.

Aidan gasped in pain, and leapt back to avoid any further injury. Light shone out from his wound, and he could feel some of his power seeping away. However, he did not have time to heal himself as Zacharias attacked again.

"I thought Asmodeus would have taught you better." Zacharias quipped.

Aidan ignored his taunt, focusing entirely on the fight. He didn't overthink his attacks, rather letting his movements flow naturally together. He watched carefully for an opening in Zacharias's defenses.

Despite the many clashes of their weapons, Zacharias did not seem to tire. Neither of them gained an advantage or weakened the other's weapon. Repeatedly, Aidan tried to reinforce his weapons with Azriel's power, but found it had no effect. Nothing he did seem to weaken Zacharias. Aidan thought back to his combat lessons with Asmodeus, and decided to change tactics. Zacharias was an Aduro, perhaps he could not be overcome with Azriel's power.

Aidan called upon the anger but rather than let it rule him, rather he allowed the emotion fuel his passion for returning home. He channeled his passion into his sword, and felt it grow stronger in his hand. Aidan renewed his attack on Zacharias with new energy. With each blow, he felt Zacharias's daggers weaken. He could see Zacharias beginning to tire, and he took advantage of it.

Across the garden, Asmodeus and Gabrielle continued to exchange blows. Despite being a formidable opponent, Asmodeus lacked his usual ferocity in combat allowing Gabrielle to keep up with him easily. Gabrielle seemed lively, and graceful in her movements, apparently unhindered by whatever taxed Asmodeus.

Her advantage was great enough that she managed to wound Asmodeus. Her swords tore through the cloth and sliced shallow wounds into his chest and arms. Her confidence only increased as the number of wounds Asmodeus bore multiplied. Becoming overly eager, Gabrielle made a foolish attack which Asmodeus sidestepped, and she exposed her back to him as her lunge carried her past him.

"You spend too much time scheming, and not enough time actually fighting." Asmodeus chided as he put some distance between them. He did not strike at her exposed back, however, too proud to take such an easy victory.

Gabrielle spun around quickly, and faced him. "Yet you are the wounded one." She answered scathingly.

"There is no shame in bearing injuries, as all experienced warriors have. You don't look like you have ever had a scratch on you." He said as he blocked another hasty strike from her.

Irritated by his remarks, Gabrielle launched into a frenzy of attacks. Asmodeus blocked each one, but he felt his sword weaken under her steady stream of attacks. However, he kept calm as he watched for another opening. Finally, his chance came, and Asmodeus stabbed at her leg. He smiled in satisfaction as the blade buried in her thigh, and she cried out.

Meanwhile, Aidan kept Zacharias from getting within striking distance again by using the protection of his shield. Finally, Aidan found the opening he was looking for as Zacharias was distracted by Gabrielle's cry. Bringing his sword forward, Aidan felt the blade slide into Zacharias's abdomen. Zacharias's weapons vanished as his power faded rapidly. Aidan could feel Zacharias's power flow into him as he faded away. He stared at the spot Zacharias had been; numbly realizing he had defeated his opponent. Aidan felt sick as he recalled how it had felt to plunge the blade into Zacharias.

However, Gabrielle's victorious laugh drew his attention back to the conflict behind him. Aidan spun around to see Asmodeus on his knees with Gabrielle's twin blades crossed at his throat. Darkness seeped from various shallow wounds, depleting Asmodeus's energy slowly. Gabrielle, on the other hand, seemed relatively unharmed aside from the wound on her leg.

"Why did I ever fear you?" She gloated triumphantly. "You are pathetic."

"Good thing I have backup," Asmodeus said in his usual smug tone despite sounding exhausted.

Aidan acted quickly as he saw Asmodeus's situation. He allowed his sword and shield to vanish. In their place, he drew a long curve in the air. Grasping the center of the arch; he joined the two ends with a thread of energy. With his bow in hand, he made the motion of notching an arrow. Aidan pulled from all of his passion and force of will to craft an arrow. He refused to fight with anger, no longer wanting the emotion to rule him. Pleased with his creation, he brought the bow and arrow up. He sighted along the arrow, and aimed its tip at Gabrielle's heart.

"Let him go, Gabrielle!" Aidan commanded.

"You wouldn't risk hitting him," Gabrielle said, remembering Aidan's presence as he spoke. She looked towards Aidan, bringing the blades closer to Asmodeus's neck.

"Want to chance it?" Aidan threatened, drawing the bowstring back further. He could see Gabrielle's hesitation, and he prayed she wouldn't call his bluff.

As Aidan provided a distraction, Asmodeus formed a dagger, and gripped it tightly. The weapon was weak, but efficient. Bringing his dagger up, Asmodeus stabbed upward, and the dagger slipped under Gabrielle's ribcage.

Gabrielle stumbled back and her swords vanished as she placed her hands around the dagger. As she moved away from Asmodeus, Aidan let the arrow fly. It flew straight and true, embedding deep in Gabrielle's chest. Her shocked expressed remained even as her energy drained, and she dissolved in the light breeze.

Aidan watched her fade away, content to let her energy be swept away. He had no desire to possess her power. Besides, he would have no need of it now that he could go home.

As Asmodeus cleared his throat, Aidan suddenly recalled his injuries. Going to Asmodeus's side, he crouched down. As he began to heal his wounds, Aidan was surprised to find that Azriel's power seemed to possess an almost endless capacity for healing, despite being less than useful for combat.

"Thanks, Aidan," Asmodeus said, sounding relieved. Aidan smiled slightly as Asmodeus used his name. Maybe he had finally earned some respect from him.

"What happened to you?" Aidan asked, still surprised by Asmodeus's injuries as he set to work healing him. "I thought you that could have won against her easily."

Asmodeus grunted as Aidan fussed over him. "She was a tough old broad." He answered in good humor, and then got to his feet as Aidan finished closing all of his wounds. "I had other obligations that required my energy. Besides, do you think maintaining that barrier was easy?" He answered defensively.

"I hope these other obligations were important enough to risk your life. She almost killed you." Aidan said critically, wondering how much energy the trap had cost Asmodeus to create. He dismissed the question, too exhausted from the fight and healing Asmodeus to pay it much thought.

"Good work getting rid of Zacharias." Asmodeus complimented.

"I wouldn't call it good work." Aidan said reluctantly, still uncomfortable with what he had done.

"I guess we can finally get you home," Asmodeus replied. "But first, someone wants to say goodbye." He said, giving a genuine smile for the first time.

"Who?" Aidan asked, giving Asmodeus a puzzled look.

Asmodeus chuckled, but would say no more. As Aidan watched, Asmodeus's mannerisms began to shift. His smile broadened, and his expression became fond with a hint of pride.

"Azriel?" Aidan asked, feeling reluctant to hope that what he was seeing was real. For a moment, he wondered if Asmodeus was playing a cruel trick.

"Hello, Aidan," Azriel said. He appeared exhausted and weak, but otherwise well.

Aidan laughed in delight, and embraced his mentor. "But how is this possible? I felt your power drain away."

"I believe Asmodeus can take the credit for ensuring my survival," Azriel explained. "As you took my power, he used his own energy to maintain my existence."

"But I thought he hated you. Why would he do that?" Aidan asked.

"He would like us to believe that he is a villain, but I think he is only fooling himself," Azriel said wisely. "Despite his behavior, Asmodeus is truly a complex being. I would never have expected him to do this, especially when it meant risking himself. Perhaps he simply respects our balance more than I anticipated."

"Is that why he almost lost to Gabrielle?"

"I imagine so. It would have taken a substantial portion of Asmodeus's energy to keep me alive once my energy was depleted. Never mind the task of constructing the barrier to keep Gabrielle from escaping." Azriel said thoughtfully. "I am surprised he managed to fight at all."

Aidan grinned, still watching Azriel with disbelief. "I'm glad you are okay Azriel." He finally said, unable to find the words to express his relief properly. "Can I tell him thank you?"

"I imagine he would find some self-satisfied comment to make, but I think he already knows how grateful we both are," Azriel said.

Aidan nodded. "I know, tell him anyway."

"Of course," Azriel replied warmly. "But now, I think it is time that you finally go home. It has been a long time in the making."

"Home." Aidan tested out the word; in disbelief that home could finally be within reach. "I think that's a great idea."

"Would you mind teleporting us to the hospital? I find my strength has yet to return." Azriel asked.

Aidan nodded, and rested his hand on Azriel's shoulder. Having such a reversal of their roles was strange. Aidan visualized his hospital room in vivid detail, eager to return home. With the vision clear in his mind, they vanished from the garden.

~~~~~~~~~

Jazz stood in a quiet corner of the hospital hallway with a police officer. Jenn had brought her a cup of tea to calm her nerves, and she clutched it tightly. She had spent the last half hour waiting for the police to arrive. The nurse whom she had seen with Aidan had vanished from the hospital quickly after being confronted.

Now she stood looking flipping through photos which the officer had pulled from the employee records. Finally, Jazz pulled out one of the photos that she recognized as the nurse. "That is definitely her." Jazz said, and handed the photo to the officer.

The policeman nodded as he took the photo. He looked up the corresponding employee record. "I'll send some uniforms to watch her apartment. I'm sure we will bring her in soon. Do you know of any reason why she might have wanted to hurt Aidan?"

Jazz thought of the ghost she had seen whispering in the nurse's ear, but knew she couldn't bring that up. "No, I've never seen her before, other than when she was working."

"Do you know if Aidan knew her?"

"I have no idea. But I don't think so." Jazz replied.

Thanks for your help." The officer said as he scribbled his final notes.

Jazz nodded. "Is there anything else I can do?" Her gaze was distracted as she noticed Aidan appear outside his hospital room door. She made brief eye contact with Aidan, but gave no other indication that she had noticed him.

"I think we are done for now. I'll need you to come to the station soon to give an official statement, but that can wait." He replied.

"Of course. Is it okay if I stay here for a while? I want to check on Aidan."

"Of course." He said, and fished out a business card from his pocket. "If there's anything else you think of, give me a call."

Jazz nodded as she took his card. "Thanks." As the officer left, she headed to the hospital room. She grinned as she saw Aidan standing by his bed, her relief evident. "You have no idea how glad I am to see you."

Aidan grinned back, equally thrilled to see her. "Hey, Jazz." He said warmly. As Jazz glanced questioningly at Azriel, he answered her unspoken question. "Sorry, this is Azriel." He explained.

"It is a pleasure to finally meet you Jazmine," Azriel said warmly.

"Nice to meet you too, Aidan has told me a lot about you. But call me Jazz, everyone does." She said, still sounding uncertain. Then she looked towards Aidan with a puzzled expression. "I thought…" Jazz said, and then let her sentence taper off. "Are you close to being able to come home? Things are getting worse here."

"I know." He answered. "But it's okay now. Gabrielle is gone now. So that I can come home." As he mentioned Gabrielle, the vivid memory of the arrow burying into her chest came to mind, and he fidgeted.

Jazz was clearly relieved to hear that he was coming home, and heard little else. "But I thought you said Azriel would have… you know, before Gabrielle let you go." Jazz said, and then blushed brightly as she looked at Azriel apologetically. "Sorry."

"No need for apologies. It was a true statement. However, to make a long story simple, Gabrielle is defeated, and Aidan can finally return home." Azriel answered, kindly leaving out Aidan's role in Gabrielle's demise as he sensed his discomfort with the topic.

Jazz's grinned at him. "That's great!"

Aidan looked just as happy as he glanced at his motionless body. "Hard to believe it's only been a few weeks." He said.

"Now it is over. I am happy for you both," Azriel said. "I only regret not having been able to send you home immediately to spare you this lengthy wait."

Aidan's excitement faded as the realization dawned that he had to leave Azriel behind. "Will I see you again?

"No," Azriel answered sadly. "It is a rare gift to be able to see into this realm." He said and glanced at Jazz with a meaningful expression. "We were lucky you were able to." He said to Jazmine.

"But if I can see you, I could always talk to Aidan for you." Jazz said quickly. "Even if he can't see you, at least he can talk with you."

"That is thoughtful of you, but I think it is best that you both move on with your mortal lives without my interference." He said, gently declining her offer. "When it is your time to pass into this realm, we may meet again. Until then, let this all be a distant memory."

Aidan watched him sadly. "You don't want to see me anymore?" He asked, sounding concerned.

"Of course, I would still like to see you, Aidan. However, it is more important that you live the life you were meant to live. You still have many things to experience. Your life has already been subject to enough tampering from our realm." Azriel answered, easing Aidan's concerns.

Aidan sighed softly. "So this is goodbye then?"

"For now," Azriel responded.

Aidan was motionless, and silent for a while, and then nodded finally. His excitement about going home was tempered by saying goodbye to Azriel. Now he truly understood what a bittersweet goodbye meant. "You'll say goodbye to Asmodeus for me too?"

"Of course, I'm sure you can imagine some clever remark from him for yourself," Azriel said. "He has never been good at farewells."

"I'm sure he would say he's glad to get rid of me." He said, realizing that he no longer felt his usual resentment for Asmodeus.

Asmodeus was difficult, but he did operate according to some moral standards, even if they were unclear. During the weeks he had spent with him, Aidan had gradually learned to respect Asmodeus, despite his reluctance to admit it. He would never have anticipated that outcome. Aidan and Azriel shared a knowing look, both aware that Asmodeus's actions spoke more clearly than his words.

"One more thing, Aidan," Azriel said, his mood growing more serious.

Aidan nodded, and waited attentively for Azriel's next statement.

"One final caution." Azriel looked at them both meaningfully. "In my experience, it is best that people not know what waits after death. Can we agree to leave it a mystery?"

Jazz and Aidan looked at each other, and then nodded in agreement. "That would be for the best," Aidan said, knowing that he wouldn't speak of his experiences with anyone, despite how much they had changed him.

"Who would believe us anyway?" Jazz asked with a good-natured smile. "Some people might believe in ghosts, but I'm not sure they are ready to hear the details of the afterlife."

Azriel chuckled in good humor. "Good."

"Azriel, what will happen with the Aduro now?"

"What do you mean?" Azriel asked.

"I mean with Gabrielle being gone. Won't the natural balance be disturbed?" He asked.

"I imagine someone will take her place. Gabrielle was powerful, and the loss will be noticed, but we can recover. The balance will be restored with time." He answered.

"Why don't you take over?" Aidan suggested. "You would be great at it."

"I appreciate your confidence in me, but I don't think it is my place. There are others who will step forward. Until then, I will ensure that Gabrielle's absence does not harm the balance."

"And what about Asmodeus?"

"I'm sure he will be happy to return to hunting Shades. That is his true calling after all. In fact, he'll be pleased that he no longer has to do Gabrielle's bidding. He can hunt as he wishes." Azriel answered.

Aidan nodded, feeling relieved. He was going home. Azriel and Asmodeus were alive and well. Even though the balance between the Aduro and Shades had suffered, it sounded promising that it would be restored.

Finally, Azriel looked towards Aidan's body. "We shouldn't delay any longer. It's time for you to return."

Slowly Aidan reached out, and touched his own hand. He no longer felt the barrier blocking him from rejoining his body. Aidan became aware of the steady beating of his heart, and the calm rhythm of his breathing. It felt so natural that he could feel his body pulling him back. He stopped himself, however and withdrew his hand.

"Is something wrong?" Azriel asked curiously.

"No, I forgot one thing," Aidan said. He held his hand out to Azriel as if reaching for a handshake.

As Azriel took his hand, Aidan spoke. "I think this power will be more useful to you. It does belong to you after all." Aidan said as he allowed Azriel's power to flow back to him. As the power vanished, he could feel a sudden void within himself. He smiled confidently, however, knowing that the power would be useless once he returned. Besides, his time with Azriel and Asmodeus had given him all the inner strength he would need to make it through any challenges his mortal life brought.

"Thank you," Azriel said, visibly strengthening as his power was returned to him. He pulled Aidan into a hug as the last of his power was returned. After embracing him for a moment, Azriel released him. With a final nod, Aidan reached out to touch his hand. This time, he did not fight the pull. He closed his eyes as he was swept into his body.

A heavy sensation overcame him, and his senses became dull. Distantly he was aware of the heart monitor's beeping, but it was muffled as if he was waking up from a deep sleep. After weeks of lying motionless, his muscles had lost their strength. With some fear he wondered if he would ever regain control. With a sense of irony, he recalled the powerful existence he had left behind, but he reassured himself with new confidence. He could overcome this.

Finally, he managed to move a finger, and he felt Jazz's gentle touch as she took his hand. Gradually he opened his eyes, and Jazz's features came into focus. He tried to smile, but could not muster the coordination. For a moment, his gaze shifted to the spot where Azriel had been standing. Aidan was disappointed, but not surprised that he could no longer see him. He looked back at Jazz, clinging to his conscious state despite the temptation to slip back into sleep.

"Welcome home." Jazz whispered. "Don't worry; you'll be strong again soon." She said reassuringly, instinctively understanding what he couldn't say.

He took a few deep breaths, trying to regain control over his foreign feeling limbs. Everything felt heavy and weak. It took him a few tries to get his muscles to begin responding.

"I love you." He whispered, his speech slurring as he formed the words awkwardly. However, Jazz seemed to understand him as she blinked away tears.

"I love you too." She said as she kissed his cheek.

Twenty-Two...

"Every day is a journey,
and the journey itself is home."
– Matsuo Basho

"Ladies and gentleman, I am pleased to present your graduating class." The valedictorian announced. As the crowd erupted into applause, the graduates stood, and threw their caps in the air.

Aidan rose slowly with the rest of the audience, applauding loudly. He watched Jazz proudly as she celebrated with the rest of the graduates. He regretted not being up on the stage with her, but knew that his time would come next year. His coma meant that he had missed too much school to be able to graduate this year. However, he was confident that he would walk across the stage next year.

With Jazz tutoring him, he hoped to achieve the marks he needed to be accepted into a good college. For the first time in his life, he was excited about his future, and had begun to make plans. He looked forward to spending his summer researching colleges, and searching for scholarships. Of course, he would also be helping Jazz prepare for college since he had insisted she not hold back on his account. After stubbornly refusing, they had compromised. Jazz would attend a local college until he was done and they could both transfer to a college of their choice.

But first, he had to finish high school. Luckily, the school had not even hesitated to prepare his schedule for the following year. They had even divided up his remaining classes to ensure he had lots of free periods so he could focus on his recovery as well.

The progress with his healing was promising as well. The doctors had commented numerous times that he had made a faster recovery than they had anticipated given the length of his coma. It had been almost two months since he had woken up, and his speech had returned to normal.

Physiotherapy had been far more painful, and lengthy, however. Aidan's progress had been slow, and frustrating despite the assurance that he was doing well. When things were painful, he swore he felt a reassuring hand on his shoulder, and a surge of renewed energy. Despite his persistent questioning, Jazz still couldn't confirm that it was Azriel's presence he had felt.

Leaning heavily on his cane, Aidan shuffled down the aisle to find Jazmine in the crowd of graduates. His mom linked her arm through his free arm, providing the extra support he needed. He smiled gratefully, and she grinned back. The joyous atmosphere was infectious.

The last couple of months had been transformational for his mom as well. It seemed that they had both found their inner strength. A few days after he had woken up, she had come in to show him the finalized the separation papers. She had even begun the process of putting a restraining order in place, forever removing Tyler from their lives. It didn't even matter what the court system did with him anymore; he wouldn't be coming back into their home again. Aidan smiled proudly as he looked at his Mom, amazed by how her strength had flourished.

As Jazz appeared out of the crowd, he took the flowers he had bought from his Mom, and handed them Jazz. "Congratulations Jazz." He said.

She beamed at him, delighted by the flowers, and hugged him. "Thanks." As she smelled the roses, she looked him over appreciatively. "Don't you look sharp in a suit? Did you wear it for me?"

"Of course." Aidan stood a little taller, feeling confident. "I think the cap, and gown suits you." He said as he playfully flicked the tassel on the cap.

Jazz laughed. "Thanks. I look forward to seeing you wear one next year."

He smiled, also looking forward to that day, but wanting to keep the attention on her accomplishment. "So Miss Graduate, where should we go to celebrate?" He asked.

Jazz didn't seem to hear him as she looked past him, staring into the crowd. Aidan glanced around, but didn't see anyone he recognized.

"Jazz?"

Jazz blinked, and looked back at him. "Sorry, I thought I saw someone we know." She answered.

"Azriel?" Aidan whispered, so his Mom wouldn't hear.

When Jazz nodded, Aidan smiled contently. "Come on; we've got a big milestone to celebrate." He said happily, fully intending to live life to the fullest as Azriel wished.

The End

About Victoria

Victoria Helmink was born and raised in the city of Victoria, British Columbia – she teases her Mother about a lack of naming creativity. A storyteller by nature, Victoria's earliest memories involve writing stories for her parents and older sister. At thirteen, she dove headlong into the love of writing and the passion has continued since. When not writing, Victoria enjoys photography, playing the piano, and reading.

Beyond Life is her first published novel. The book was inspired by a dream about a young boy and an unwilling mentor.

If you want to stay in touch and read more visit:
www.victoriahelmink.com
www.facebook.com/VictoriaHelmink